Gold
Dust

Gold Dust

Ibrahim al-Koni

Translated by
Elliott Colla

Arabia Books
London

First published in Great Britain in 2008 by
Arabia Books
26 Cadogan Court
Draycott Avenue
London SW3 3BX
www.hauspublishing.co.uk

This edition published by arrangement with
The American University in Cairo Press
113 Sharia Kasr el Aini, Cairo, Egypt
420 Fifth Avenue, New York, NY 10018
www.aucpress.com

First published in Arabic in 1990 as *al-Tibr*
Copyright © 1990 by Ibrahim al-Koni
The moral right of the author has been asserted
Protected under the Berne Convention

English translation copyright © 2008 by Elliott Colla

ISBN 978-1-906697-02-0
Printed in Egypt
1 2 3 4 5 6 7 8 9 10   14 13 12 11 10 09 08

Cover design: Arabia Books
Design: AUC Press

Gold
Dust

For that which befalleth the sons of men befalleth beasts; even
one thing befalleth them: as the one dieth, so dieth the other;
yea, they have all one breath; so that a man hath no preemi-
nence above a beast: for all is vanity. All go unto one place; all
are of the dust, and all turn to dust again.

Ecclesiastes 3:19–20

Among those owing fealty to the sultan of this kingdom are the
peoples of the deserts of gold dust. The heathen savages who
live there bring him gold each year, and when the sultan
wishes, he seizes them as his slaves. But as the rulers of this
kingdom know from experience, no sooner do they conquer
one of these cities than the gold begins to dwindle. No sooner
do they establish Islam there, and no sooner does the call to
prayer go out, than the gold dries up completely. Meanwhile,
throughout the neighboring heathen countries, the gold contin-
ues to grow and grow.

Ibn Fadlallah al-'Umari (1301–1349)
The Kingdom of Mali and its Surroundings

When Ukhayyad received the camel as a gift from the chief of the Ahaggar tribes, he was still a young colt. Back then, on moonlit nights, Ukhayyad liked to brag about the thoroughbred camel to the other young men of the tribe, taking pleasure in posing questions to himself and then answering them.

"Have any of you ever seen a piebald Mahri before?"

"Never!"

"Have you ever seen a thoroughbred so graceful, so light of foot and so well proportioned?"

"Not until now."

"Have you ever seen a Mahri who could compete with him in pride, fierceness, and loyalty?"

"Not like this one."

"Have you ever seen a gazelle who took on the form of a camel?"

"Of course not."

"Did you ever see anything more beautiful or noble?

"No, no, no! Admit it—you've never seen such a thing before and you never will again!" He would leap into the open skipping

5

like a dancing madman until, exhausted, he would collapse on his back on the sand. There, he would raise his voice, singing one of those bewitching songs, like charms against loneliness that riders take refuge in whenever they travel across waterless deserts. He would sing his sad ballad and close with well-known lines taken from the epic of Amud's war against the French invasion of the desert:

How well did we receive Amud when he approached!
We gave him thoroughbreds dressed for war
And lent him riders who never miss their mark . . .

Ukhayyad's passion for the piebald thoroughbred grew so intense that he finally sought out a famous poetess of the Kel Abada tribes. He asked her to compose a poem glorifying the Mahri's innate qualities and extolling his talents, likening him to warrior heroes.

All night long the young man sat enumerating the qualities of the piebald: "He's piebald. He's graceful and long legged. He's well bred. He's fierce and loyal."

"It's not wrong for a rider to laud the qualities of his mount or to sing about him like an angel," the experienced poetess abruptly interrupted. "But when you decide to commit praise to verse, you must follow convention. Poetry has its rules, after all! Your Mahri has never raised a battle cry nor made a name for himself at dancing festivals."

Confused, Ukhayyad tried to hide his embarrassment behind his veil. "But he's piebald," he blurted out. "It's enough that he's piebald. Did you ever see a piebald Mahri before?"

In the past, he had entrusted the vassals of the tribe with the job of breaking in the Mahri and getting him used to the bridle. But that had to change now—it would be wrong for him to rely on vassals to teach him to dance too. In the desert, only noblemen trained camels to dance in front of the womenfolk.

2

Before entering the ring, Ukhayyad wanted to fit out the camel in style. He borrowed most of the necessities, from the saddle and saddlecloth to the bridle, reins, bag, and even the whip. His old dressings were pale and dull-colored, bleached by the sun and unfit for adorning a Mahri that was preparing to dance in front of women, swaying back and forth to the rhythm and melody of music.

He spent an entire day fitting out his equipage. The saddle had been crafted by the cleverest of the Ghat smiths. The dressing was an embroidered kilim rug brought from Touat by merchants. The bridle had been braided by old women of the Ifoghas tribe in Ghadamès. The travel bag had been stitched by the fingers of Tamenrasset noblewomen. The whip was a rare piece, covered by strips of leather on which hands in Kano had once engraved magical charms. After the whip played its role in bringing about Ukhayyad's disgrace, some elders guessed that it had been supplied to him by the envious young men of the tribe.

He entered the clearing after noon. In the small valley, the women sat in a circle around their drums. The younger women made a wider ring around them. The sheikhs took their place on the rise to the south, the men and boys stood across from them, their heads wrapped in lavish blue turbans. When they strode, they swaggered with the pride of peacocks. The Mahri thorough-breds were hitched together in a long line on the two sides of the open space, one set to the west, another, facing it, fixed to the east.

Soon a wedding procession made its way into the valley. The celebration was for one of the tribe's vassals—a habitual divorcer and marrier who had decided this time to take a beautiful mulatta, choosing to savor the taste of Tuareg blood mixed with the heat of Africans.

The entertainment now began with the secondary formations.

Two sleek riders from the western line went first, then two set off opposite them from the east. They met beside the dance arena and galloped off to a torrent of ululations.

Ukhayyad got ready. Beside him gleamed one of the vassal youths, crowned with a Tagolmost turban and girthed with a shiny leather belt. He sat on an elaborately decorated saddle that rested firmly on the back of an elegant gray Mahri camel. This youth would accompany him as he went across the field.

The two approaching men from the other side drew near. The youth sidled his camel up to the piebald Mahri. "It's my proud honor to escort you today." He smiled. "There's no purebred like your piebald throughout the whole desert." An eye winked behind thick blue fabric. The gesture unnerved Ukhayyad. He saw nothing sincere in the eyes of his companion.

They began to move.

They paced in unison, with firm, arrogant strides, pushing the other camel on, moving in harmony. In the short space that separated the emptiness stretching to the west from the singing circle in the middle, Ukhayyad experienced a lifetime of happiness.

The two thoroughbreds moved in unison, their approach slow and balanced. Ukhayyad felt that he was flying on wings in the air, his heart nearly bursting from the enchantment, anxiety, and hidden joy of the moment. Possessed by the music, he lived as hostage to the dance, its passion, and mysterious longing. He guessed that the magnificent piebald shared these same wrenching sensations as they went along to the circle, though he could not say how.

He awoke from the dream to find his partner had swaggered off to the east, toward the line of riders. For his part, the piebald had veered instead to the left, and turned back upon the dancing arena. The girls in the circle laughed among themselves. Mortified, Ukhayyad took the enchanted whip into hand, hoping to drive the camel back into formation. But as soon as the piebald felt the blow of the whip on his skin, he went mad. Instead of moving toward the right or rejoining his partner, he kicked at the circle of girls, then lost his mind altogether. Ukhayyad whipped his flanks again, but the beast's madness only grew fiercer. He rushed directly into the women's circle, smashing a handsome drum covered with gazelle skin. The women scattered and the singing came to a halt. Then all was commotion. Ukhayyad pulled the reins until the neck of the mad thoroughbred arched backwards between his legs. But even reining him like that did not stop his frenzied motion across the dance arena. He continued to kick at everything in his path, frothing at the mouth and champing wildly at the bit.

Froth began to fly all over the women in gleaming sprays. Then a throng of strong men on foot hurried over and caught him in ropes. The piebald struggled against them too, so that they were forced to knock him down.

Together, Ukhayyad and the piebald were thrown to the ground on the dance arena.

3

hat was not the first time.

The camel had entangled Ukhayyad in far worse humiliations many times before. In the past, he had been in the habit of embarking on late night romantic forays into the nearby encampments. He would saddle up the camel after sunset and depart for his lover's camp, to arrive only after midnight. He would tether the thoroughbred in the nearest valley and then steal through the shadows to the ladies' tents. There, he would flirt and chat all night, stealing kisses until the first light broke on the horizon of the desert. Then he would slip back to the valley, leap into saddle, and rush headlong home.

These forays kept up until he realized that his graceful camel had himself become smitten with a lovely she-camel owned by a tribe that spent each spring in the valley of Magharghar. Ukhayyad used to visit a beautiful daughter of that noble clan. He let the piebald graze in the valley floor with the herd while he dallied with the girl in her tents. The tender feelings of his Mahri had not gone unnoticed by him. In fact, from the first visit, he had recognized his steed's passion for a white she-camel. He became more certain about it after he saw how the piebald flew to Magharghar, seeming to burn with longing for night travel. Ukhayyad gave him a hard time, asking, "Why hide it from me? Admit it—you're not racing me toward my beloved, you're flying to get to yours! Admit it—there's no reason for you to rush there this time. There must be a female behind it. Women are always the reason!"

Leaning forward, spitting, and chewing at his bridle in his joyous rush, the thoroughbred would respond, "Aw-a-a-a-a-a-a." And Ukhayyad would laugh and slap him.

Then came the day the broom trees burst into bloom with their sad white flowers. He tethered the camel in the valley and left him to graze next to the fragrant broom, not realizing that broom blossoms were a sign that spring had come to the desert valleys. And when spring arrives, it brings with it the mating season—and madness seizes the beasts and sends them into a frenzy. That is what happened on that day.

Ukhayyad had only been murmuring in the girl's ear a short while when he heard the roar of the rutting beast. At first, he thought it was distant thunder, and he went on stroking her face and flirting. The roar repeated itself even more furiously. He leaped from the tent and rushed to the valley. There, the piebald was crashing into a ferocious gray camel in a terrible battle. Their fight, of course, was over a she-camel. As the dawn split the horizon, the Mahri's wounds appeared in the feeble light. His opponent's teeth had shredded his neck and lower jaw and had seriously wounded his left thigh. But the horrible gray adversary had also been wounded, and was bleeding profusely. His entire body was covered in blood.

The commotion awoke the whole tribe. Shepherds rushed into the valley armed with sticks. It was only after a long struggle that they managed to separate the two opponents. The sun burst forth and Ukhayyad realized he had been caught, completely exposed. When the tribe's young men arrived at the scene, he could sense their scorn. Their eyes told him that they knew everything. Then they led him to the sheikh of the tribe, a tall, lean, old man who held an elegant cane made of lote wood crowned by leather straps embossed with delicate patterns.

Deep wrinkles laced his cheeks, though his glance radiated lively health and an enigmatic sense of mischief. He ordered tea to be prepared and indicated that Ukhayyad should sit down on the kilim inside the tent. He then turned the lote wood cane over in his hands before finally speaking. "There's no shame in a noble man being in love, or embarking on journeys to clandestine meetings. But what's wrong with abiding by Muslim law and entering houses by their front doors?"

He smiled and added, "It delights us to receive the son of the sheikh of Amanghasatin in our parts. He earned the honor of having stopped the foreign attackers and halting their intrusion into the desert."

Ukhayyad understood that the clever sheikh intended to smooth things over and calm the young men with his talk about romantic adventures, and his gesture to the role Ukhayyad's father had played in repelling foreign invaders from the Sahara. Tribal sheikhs never utter a single word they do not mean—and they express themselves through allusion rather than plain speech.

One of his men brought out the piebald, now exhausted from his injuries. He was covered in blood and spit and sweat and dust.

The astute sheikh took in the mark and build of the camel, then called to his men, "My God! What is this?! Why didn't you tell me that our noble guest possessed a thoroughbred of such perfection? He's a piebald Mahri as graceful as a gazelle. This line became extinct throughout the desert a hundred years ago. By God, where did you come by him?"

Glad for the chance to cover himself, Ukhayyad said, "From the chieftain of the Ahaggar. He gave it to me when I reached manhood."

"Ahh. The chief of the Ahaggar. Ibrahim Bakda. This is a kind of animal that befits a hero like him. No one but he could give such a gift. Those old tribes—they've always got surprises and secrets.

"We always say that the Mahri is the mirror of his rider. If you want to stare into the rider and see what lies hidden within, look to his mount, his thoroughbred. Now that I look at you more closely, I can see you're a young man who's got everything. Whoever owns a Mahri like this piebald will never complain for want of noble values. You've honored our homes, O noble youth descended from noble men!

"But I'm sorry to say, you have little chance of inheriting your father's position in the tribe. From what I know, your father has three nephews, each of whom is more ready to take over than you . . . . But who knows? Maybe a miracle will happen. The door to miracles is always open."

A gigantic youth with grim cheeks and rough hands began to serve the first round of green tea.

The sheikh blew on the head of foam on the tea. He placed his cup on the ground and said, "Our noble guest should also allow us to treat his Mahri with generosity. Riders often grumble about having to enter our homes through the front door. But there's no harm in his thoroughbred doing that."

He smiled and most of those present smiled along with him. Ukhayyad did not understand the signal. He could not grasp what the sheikh was alluding to. The sheikh continued aloud, "A rider might escape the women of the tribe, but a rare thoroughbred shouldn't be allowed to escape its she-camels. I see how our she-camels want to claim him as their own. Having piebald Mahris among our herds will be the envy of all the tribes. It's our duty to resuscitate the piebald line and preserve it from extinction. What does our guest think?"

The sheikh did not wait for his guest's opinion. He ordered that she-camels be brought before the Mahri. That day, Ukhayyad witnessed for the first time how males impregnate females. They led in a white she-camel and forced her to her knees on the open ground. They hobbled her fore and hind legs. Then they led the rutting piebald to her and gathered around them. The camel kneeled down on top of her until it seemed to Ukhayyad that the poor she-camel's ribs would break. She frothed and squealed and vomited frothing spit. When her tail blocked him from entering, one of the men wrenched it out of the way. The wailing rattled the houses, causing the women and children to come out and gape. In front of the houses, they lined up in deep rows. Every now and then the old man would chuckle and point his cane into the air, repeating, "The rider might fly, but this piebald shall not."

The whole operation was awful. Whenever Ukhayyad remembered it, he was filled with fury and embarrassment.

4

The camel continued his adventures in desert pastures where she-camels roamed loose. But eventually his blind virility cost him. One day he returned, the spark of mischief extinguished from his large eyes, his bottom lip drooping. He stood on the open desert, still and silent, casting a sad gaze across a horizon that danced and flickered with tongues of a celestial mirage.

Ukhayyad noticed the camel's sullenness, but for some days did not discover the reason. He was inspecting the camel's lustrous coat, checking for ticks and pulling out a lote thorn from his speckled skin. There, on his hide, beneath the pelt, a disease and inflammation had taken hold. He scratched at it with his fingers and the Mahri winced and bellowed in pain. He brought out the shears and chose a place to cut away the thick hair. Underneath, the beast's skin had turned black and the flesh had been eaten away.

In the coming days, he saw that the mange was spreading and devouring new spots on the piebald's body. He went to the wise men of the tribe, the doctors, asking for advice. They agreed that there was little hope for a cure: "When mange takes hold of a camel, expect the worst." But Ukhayyad did not lose faith. He could not allow himself to believe that there was a power capable of stealing his piebald from him. One blind man, an expert of animal diseases, shook his head and answered him skeptically: "Son—after laughter come tears. Just as sorrow follows happiness, so too does death intrude into the foolishness of life."

But the young man would not be reconciled. The piebald was not a mortal creation. Ukhayyad recalled how he cared for his steed and how he had raised the camel after receiving him, still a colt, from the great chieftain. During famine, he would sneak barley from the tent, placing it in the palms of his hands to offer it to the camel. His secret was soon discovered and the black servant woman complained about it to his mother. This was all before his mother had died. His mother told his father, who scolded him, saying, "At a time when not everybody has grain to eat, you go and give it to the livestock!" That day he answered his father: "The piebald is not livestock. The piebald is the piebald." His father, who hardly ever smiled, chuckled and shook his finger at the boy, perhaps pleased by the cleverness of the boy's answer.

In those days the young Mahri would wander with Ukhayyad from tent to tent, following on his heels like a dog. He would trot after him, even when he went to stay out at all-night gatherings in barren regions, and he would not sleep until Ukhayyad had lain down first. He even escorted the young man when he wandered into the desert to relieve himself. These things made Ukhayyad's cohort laugh at him, but he did not care. He submitted to the caresses and tendernesses of the camel and retorted: "Sheikh Musa says that animals are superior to humans and make the best friends. I heard him say that." Sheikh Musa was a man who read books and recited the Qur'an and led the people in prayer. He was all alone in the world, without wife, children, or relatives, and wandered around with the tribe even though he was not of the tribe. It was said he came from the western ends of the desert, from Fez, the land of teachers and scholars of Islamic law. Sheikh Musa was the one who whispered to him the secret that saved his piebald: "This must stay between us, but only silphium can cure your camel. Don't be an idiot, listen to what I say. Go to the desolate fields of Maimoun next spring. Since the fall of Rome, silphium grows nowhere but there. Secure the Mahri well so he cannot escape and let him graze one or two days. You'll see." Then he repeated enigmatically, "But don't forget to secure him well."

Among the tribe, silphium was another name for the fury of jinn and madness itself. Whoever tasted it, whether beast or man, lost their senses and went mad. Dread of this legendary plant was passed down from generation to generation. As soon as a child became mature enough to herd goats, he was told, "Don't graze the goats in the fields of Maimoun. There's silphium there. There may be a thousand cures in that weed, but each one passes by the door of jinn. If silphium takes to you, it will cure you of any ailment. But what is the use of restoring health if you then lose your wits? He who loses his reason has lost his soul!" His mother had recited this very warning when he had grown old enough to herd the goats in the valleys.

Sheikh Musa's injunction frightened him. Would the piebald really become possessed? Would he lose his wits?

And how exactly does an animal lose his reason? Do his eyes bulge and turn bloodshot? Does froth drool from his lips? Does he beat his head against stones like men who have become slaves to passion during late-night revelries, or like dervishes who join the Sufi brotherhoods and rove through the encampments and deserts, beating tambourines and wandering all night, every night?

This would be a fate more wretched than mange. Rather than submitting to the sage's advice, Ukhayyad roamed the encampments searching for others knowledgeable in animal diseases. He could not bear seeing his steed suffer the cruelty of the other shepherds. They had separated him from the camel herd, fearing the contagion, and left him to graze, isolated and alone in the pastures. Ukhayyad preferred to accompany him in his tribulation, setting out with him in the pastures from dawn, not returning until night. Sometimes, Ukhayyad himself was harsh with the Mahri and scolded him, "This is all the result of your recklessness. What have you gained now from your adventures? Didn't you listen to what Sheikh Musa said, 'Females are the most dangerous trap males can fall into.' Adam was led astray by his woman and God condemned him to be expelled from the Garden. If it were not for that damn woman, us men would have remained there, blessed with an easy life, left to wander freely about paradise.

"There are serpents and scorpions lurking in every hole, ready to sting any idiot who sticks a limb in. What did your sweet she-camel do to you? It turns out she was also a serpent. She's lovely, but she bites. And the germ you carry is the price of it. You must bear your situation and be patient for the time being."

The beast lowered his eyelids and answered in shame, "Aw-a-a-a-a-a-a."

"Oh, *now* you regret it," Ukhyayyad smiled bitterly. "Regret won't do you any good. What will we do with your disease? Don't you understand how serious this is? Mange is more contagious than smallpox or the plague. God save us from it. Don't you know, life contains nothing but pitfalls and traps. If you don't pay attention to where you put your foot, you'll step right into one. Good God—it was I who raised you to become so heedless! Your mother didn't get to enjoy seeing you as an adult when the great chief brought you to me. But tell me, by God, how am I supposed to enlighten your mind if I myself, no less than you, need someone to enlighten me? Living blindfolded is our lot, and only traps can teach us wisdom. How reckless we are!"

The Mahri drew near and nuzzled Ukhayyad with his shoulder. Ukhayyad regretted his tirade and changed his tone: "It does not matter. Don't worry. Thoughtless she-camels may have infected you, but pay them no mind. We'll find a way out. We have to find a way. Just be patient. You must be very patient if you want to get out of this mess. Life consists of nothing but patience, as old men say."

He held the Mahri's head in his embrace and stood there, consoling and consoling him in the pasture.

A righteous man regardeth the life of his beast: but the tender mercies of the wicked are cruel.

Proverbs 12:10

5

While traveling through the various encampments, Ukhayyad acquired some thick salve from the Bouseif tribes. He sheared the piebald's fleece and massaged the blackened skin with it three times a day. This soon made the skin supple. But the blackness continued to consume the camel's body, creeping ever lower, wrapping around the belly and eating at the legs. Another man knowledgeable in animal diseases arrived with a caravan of merchants from Aïr. He gave Ukhayyad a dark ointment in a small vial and told him he had distilled it from herbs. Ukhayyad applied the medication until it ran out. A few weeks later, the blackened skin began to peel off. Blood oozed profusely, but the scabs would not congeal. Ukhayyad could not bear to see the threads of blood that trickled from the piebald's body. In the eyes of others, he saw pity and sympathy. But the sympathy was only for him, not the afflicted beast.

By now the piebald was no longer piebald. The lustrous speckles had disappeared from his gray body. The keen glance had faded from his beguiling eyes. His lean, graceful frame had been transformed into a bloated and splotched skeleton. He was now the pale and wretched image of his former self. God may create, but disease can transform His creations into completely other beings. And as with beasts, so too with humans.

The piebald would no longer go near him in the light of day. The camel spent his hours chasing angels whose flight shimmered in the mirages on the horizon. He was embarrassed when Ukhayyad showed him affection in public, so much so that when the young man came to rub him with medicine, the Mahri would dodge and try to flee. Sometimes he would complain miserably, "Aw-a-a-a-a-a."

It was only with the shadows of the night that the piebald would sneak up on him, long after everything in the desert had faded and died down. In the deep darkness, when only jinn moved across the open wastes, murmuring among each other in secret conversation, the miserable piebald crept up and nuzzled his head against the blankets of his friend. Ukhayyad, sleepless with anxiety, was trying to steal a short spell before dawn shot its light at the horizon. The camel nudged at the covers. He prodded at the exposed parts of Ukhayyad's body with fleshy lips. Then he thrust his long head under the blanket. With a groan, Ukhayyad embraced him, and together the two wept, each licking away the tears of the other, tasting the salt and the pain. When the shadows of death descend, this is all creatures can do. Ukhayyad turned his eyes toward the pale, shamefaced moon and sighed, "Why does God create if death must follow birth? Why must His creatures suffer before they die?" Then he bit his lip: "God damn women!"

One day, he grew sick of complaining. In the evening, beneath the covers so that no other creature would hear them,

Ukhayyad told his friend, "That's enough. We've had our fill of suffering. We need to do something, even if it's madness. We'll try Sheikh Musa's plan. Islamic scholars from Fez are wise — everyone in the desert knows that. Even if the price is madness, what's so wrong for a creature to lose his senses? Don't you see — we're going to go crazy whether we eat silphium or not! I don't want to watch any longer as your body falls apart piece by piece. I will go insane before you die that way. Yes, that way, you will die and I will be the one who loses his mind. Now can you see what small moments of carelessness can cost?"

With that resolve, Ukhayyad traveled with the camel to the merciful western Hamada desert, heading toward the ancient pagan shrine nestled within its mountains. He never realized that had he delayed his travel even days longer, his father would have taken matters into his own hand and killed the sick animal. The man had been planning to end the mangy thoroughbred's misery by putting a bullet in its head.

6

At the entrance to where the two mountains faced one another, in an open waste that stretched on forever, stood the shrine of the Magus, tucked into the folds of a lonely hillside. In the past, the tomb had had frequent visitors, even religious teachers and scholars. No one had considered it an idolatrous object. Everyone agreed that it belonged to a Muslim from Arabia who had been witness to the early Islamic conquests, a companion of the Prophet who had died of thirst in the desert while fighting on behalf of God's religion. Nomads of the desert sought out the saint, sometimes visiting the monument alone, sometimes coming in large groups. They would sacrifice animals to him, spilling the blood of their offerings before the shrine. That was until the pagan soothsayer from Kano arrived. 'The crow' as people called him, was an old black man who wore a necklace of river oyster shells around his leathered neck. On his head, he wore a black turban, and his silky, broad robes were of the same color. The man traveled alone on an emaciated she-camel, and stayed away from other people. He chewed tobacco and would spit in the faces of curious children and people who got too close. It was this fearsome witch doctor who first demolished the myth of the shrine.

The stone base of the shrine was triangular. At the top, the image of the god was set into the body of a large stone. Its neckless head sat directly on the torso. Its enigmatic features suggested it had been worshiped for millennia. Only rocks accustomed to receiving supplications over the eons could ever take on such features. The idol evoked tenderness and harshness, mercy and vengeance, wisdom and arrogance, and above all, patience—the patience of immortals well acquainted with the treachery of time and the loneliness of existence. The god's right eye and cheek had been devoured by a millennium of dust and sand blown by the hot southern winds. The left side, in contrast, still bore testimony to the sad history of the desert. It faced the northern mountain, looking heavenward toward a peak that was wrapped in a pale blue turban. The remains of ancient bones lay scattered around the idol. Some had crumbled, while the vestiges of others—other animal sacrifices—remained intact.

The witch doctor had undone the myth of the shrine by reading the symbols engraved on the pedestal of the idol. He said they spelled the name of an ancient Saharan god. He went on to decipher the ancient Tifinagh alphabet, but he refused to reveal the hidden truth that had been buried at the feet of the god. Months later, he was found dead in a nearby plain. No one had ever been able to get him to disclose the secret of the pagan talismans.

At the shrine, Ukhayyad forced the splotched piebald to kneel. He stood there a long time, attempting to divine the secrets of the desert from the structure of the inscrutable idol. Finally, he prostrated himself, raised his hands and cried, "O lord of the desert, god of the ancients! I promise to offer up to you one fat camel of sound body and mind. Cure my piebald of his malignant disease and protect him from the madness of silphium! You are the all hearing, the all knowing." He poured dust from the shrine all over the Mahri's half-consumed body, then lay down and slept until the desert burst forth with the light of dawn. He made a cup of green tea, then made his way to the desolate western pastures.

That night, he had dreamed that the piebald was drowning in the valley. A flash flood swept over and swallowed him up. Ukhayyad clutched at the camel's reins and fought the cold water. He tore at the animal from one side, while the torrent tugged at the Mahri from the other. The camel stumbled onto its front knees more than once, then sank beneath the violent waters until his head went under. Ukhayyad resisted the water's pull, yanking at the halter from the other end. Blood poured from the nostrils of the struggling beast. Had he torn the muzzle at the bridle? The struggle went on for a long time—a very long time—until the fury calmed and the dark waters began to recede across the roaring valley. To his astonishment, he saw that the murky water had been transformed into demons who, like the water, were pulling at the Mahri by the tail, intent on dragging the animal into a dark abyss. Ukhayyad awoke from the nightmare to see the first blaze as it pierced the twilight of dawn.

He thought a long time about this sign. Dreams at shrines call for the expertise of soothsayer interpretation. Sheikh Musa was well versed in the kinds of visions that took place around Muslim saints' tombs. But only the witch doctors of Kano had the special competence to read visions inspired by ancient tombs, pagan tombs. Kano soothsayers often traveled with merchant caravans in the desert—but where could Ukhayyad find one? One could not treat the revelations of shrines lightly. To seek out the knowledge of scholars at any cost was no less a duty in Muslim law than pursuing holy war. That is what the sheikhs said. But where could he find a scholar of shrines in this empty waste? Where would he come across someone who knew how to read the signs of heathen idols?

His maternal grandfather had been wise in these matters. Whenever he had dreamed, he would not rise from his bed until they brought him soothsayers who could interpret the dream for him. The whole tribe remembered how he liked to say, "If God ever sends you a warning, and its secret is revealed to you, you must pause and take heed. If you do not, you will have no one but yourself to blame." He was a firm believer in the treachery of two things—time and people—and neither failed to disappoint. No misdeed ever surprised him, nor did any enemy ever catch him off guard. Everyone agreed that his wisdom sprang entirely from the attention he paid to occult signs. It was said that even death did not take him by surprise. One night, he dreamed of the fabled lote tree, said by some tribes to exist in the middle of the western desert next to the spring whose waters grant immortality. In his dream, he drank from that pool. In the morning, the soothsayer told him, "Ready yourself for a journey. What you have seen is the lote tree at the furthest reaches of existence." So he prepared his burial shroud, washed his body with ritual care, and donned his finest clothing, then waited for the King of Death. He did this each day for a week after the dream, until he breathed his last.

7

Thick purple clouds hung above the fields of Maimoun cleaving to the peaks of the mountains, then receding into the endless desert void. While each mountain rose separately out of the surrounding desolation, together they effected a wall that split the desert in two. Across the spaces between the lone summits rolled a sea of rich, red soil, where grew patches of grass and wild flowers whose sweet odor filled the air. It was the end of spring, but the sun was not yet overpowering. Ukhayyad gathered a good number of desert truffles and killed a snake with his stick. Then he began to search in earnest for the herb the sheikh had promised. Toward sunset, he found an entire field of the fabled plants—each stood a meter in height with dark green leaves. The branches of the plant dangled low to the ground, revealing magical, delicate stalks. At the top of each stem opened a yellow bud that gave off a dark, musky scent—the flower of jinn!

Repressing his own shudders and misgivings at the fruit of generations of myth and terror, he led the camel toward the field, where he hobbled the camel's forelegs with thick palm rope. He secured the bridle to the camel's tail, letting the rope hang slack so his neck could move freely while he grazed. Ukhayyad stood there, thinking, trying to remember how the jinn in such places plotted their schemes. He told himself, "Old women say with confidence that jinn are not like humans. There's no deception and no trickery with jinn. The kernel of their difference lies in their dignity. If there were a contest over who was more dignified, man or jinn, the latter would win. If you wrong a jinn, he'll respond in kind. If you treat him right, he'll do the same. Jinn do not know how to deceive, they play by the rules. The important thing is to always be aware of your own motives and actions toward them."

The hungry animal began to devour the jinn plant, filling his mouth, raising his head toward the horizon, then chewing for a long time before swallowing what was in his mouth.

Ukhayyad stood still, watching him until nightfall. He lit a fire and roasted the truffles on the coals. He continued to observe the piebald, but saw no change of behavior. Sated, the camel kneeled on the green field, and was absorbed again in chewing the taboo herb. To Ukhayyad, it seemed as if the spark had returned to the animal's eyes. Life had returned to the dead sockets. He could not completely make out the pupils in the darkness, but the hale, alert, and steady glance flashed again and again by the light of the fire.

The shadows intensified, and silence descended, a silence unbroken by anything but the sounds of the piebald as he chomped on the cud of the magical herb. Using his arm for a pillow, Ukhayyad lay down and went to sleep.

He passed the night in broken fits of sleep, the anticipation of surprise keeping him from a more restful slumber.

In the morning, Ukhayyad looked closely at his friend, who on waking became active, jerking his head back and forth in agitation. Yesterday's spark was no illusion. A flash really had returned to his shiny eyes, displacing their former sadness. God be praised—was this the harbinger of health? Or was it a sign suggesting the onslaught of insanity? Where was the madness? Wasn't it tied to the cure? If the animal didn't lose his mind, how could he hope to be healed? Mustn't reason depart if vigor was to return? Good God! But Ukhayyad did not lose hope. Miracles often happened in the desert, and he was not asking for a large one. He was asking the jinn of the silphium fields only this: to take his friend's suffering and spare him. He prayed and pleaded incessantly. The tomb of the old saint would not let him down. He would not lose hope. Still, where was your magic, silphium? Where was your spell, your effect? Was the spark in the piebald's eyes a sign? A sign of something. One had to heed signs. As in his dream, as in all inscrutable visions. These signs were the language of God. The one who ignored them would be damned in this world. Whoever paid them no attention would receive what was coming to him. God protect us from that!

The sparkle in the eyes had indeed been a hidden sign. The following day, the battle erupted. It began in the late afternoon. The Mahri stood frightened, stiffening his tail, then began to whip it as if he were chasing imaginary flies. Then his ears began to twitch and his black skin began to quiver and tremble. He tried to unfetter his front legs. The spark in his eyes had become desperate. Ukhayyad readied himself, though he did not know what to do. Anxious as the piebald, he watched as the animal began to chomp at the air and spit up white spume. The foam rose up around his lips, then began to fall to the ground in large, frothy clusters. The raw skin dripped sweat. Ukhayyad had never seen such profuse, searing sweat on the skin of a camel as he did on that day. Then the Mahri began to stand up, trying to break the cords around his legs. He cried out with a horrible gurgling sound that pricked Ukhayyad's heart. He ran to the camel, struggling to calm him, stroking his body. "Patience, patience. Life is but patience," he repeated mechanically. "Don't we have an agreement? If you remain patient, you'll be cured. I know the jinn are powerful. But patience is even stronger than they are." But the Mahri was not patient. He howled out a long, pained complaint, "Aw-a-a-a-a-a."

The echo of his cry rebounded between the isolated peaks that stretched across the endless waste. Like a needle, the sound buried itself in Ukhayyad's heart. He gently massaged the camel's neck where perspiration continued to pour out. And now froth rather than sweat began to seep from the black skin, saturating it in an intense white lather. The camel collapsed on his front knees, then jerked up again. Clearly, the pain in his belly was unbearable—and he could not stand still in any position or place. His head jerked back as he stood up. Then blood began to spill from his nostrils where the bridle joined the nose ring.

Ukhayyad whispered, "Ay—don't try to do that again. You'll split your muzzle wide open. You'll destroy yourself. Be patient. Patience. Brave warriors can tread across coals without shedding a tear. They know how to walk through fire without complaint. Just bear the fire in your belly for one or two nights, then you'll be cured of your disease forever. Agreed?"

The Mahri would not listen to his pleadings. For good reason—*He whose foot is in the fire hears nothing*, as they say.

Ukhayyad leaped into the open desert and prayed: "Go easy, Lord! Be gentle! Lord, give him strength to face the jinn." He returned and wiped the lather off the piebald, addressing him. "What wouldn't I do for you? If I could, I'd share your pain. But God created us as we are, weak and impotent. No one can bear someone else's pain for them."

He turned away and cried out, "Lord, divide his share of pain. Let me be the one to lighten his burden. He has already suffered so much. It is not fair that he should suffer by himself all these months—he is mute and unable to express his complaint. But he comprehends. And he feels pain, excruciating pain—otherwise he would not be howling. Purebred creatures do not cry out unless the pain is unbearable. Take away some of his load and place it on my shoulders. He's carried me on his back for years, so why can't I carry his burden for just a few hours? Why shouldn't I bear his cares for just a few days?"

In the white lather on his skin, blood and pus now mixed with sweat. Black sweat and black water—the black torrent of his dream. Was this now also a vision?

The beast continued trying to escape. The rope dug a deep gash in his forelegs, and the blood ran down his shins. Above his foot, the front hobble loosened and the palm rope broke apart. Ukhayyad leaped toward him, grabbing the reins. The beast opened his jaws as far as they would go, and froth, mucous and black bile spilled out. Ah, black bile—sign of the evil eye. The soothsayers all agree on that. So, he had been envied for his piebald. The evil eye had been behind everything that had happened. According to the teaching of soothsayers, envy is stronger than poison. And the eye of the envier is deadlier than a poisoned arrow, the blow of a sword, or the thrust of a dagger. It's deadlier than any weapon. So when did the envious thugs cast their eye on him? The Mahri split the silence of the waste: "Aw-a-a-a-a-a-a."

The cry rent the never-ending horizon. The desert reverberated with it, echo upon echo, before it was swallowed up again by the transcendent silence.

Ukhayyad became frantic, moving about and talking without knowing what he was saying. "Enough already. The jinn have possessed him. Endure the jinn, and you'll triumph over them. Patience. Patience is life itself."

Yet Ukhayyad maintained his grip on the reins. "Lord, will he die? And what will I do if he does?" he called out one more time. "My God—You gave me the most loyal friend and now You're taking him from me like this, between one day and the next, leaving me to face my enviers by myself? Don't take him from me, Lord! You are not cruel, Lord. You are ever merciful. You . . . ."

A flood of tears poured from his eyes, hot as embers. He felt the fire in his eyes, and sighed. "If it must be done, then take me with him. Take us together."

At that moment, the Mahri bolted, snatching Ukhayyad up off the ground. The camel galloped across the empty waste. Together they ran. Ukhayyad clung to the reins, trying, without much success, to steer the piebald and to return him to his senses.

On the horizon to the far west, a purple shroud of thin clouds wrapped themselves around a lonely mountain summit. Behind it, the sun began to disappear and die.

The camel rushed for that mountain. He crossed a plain thick with wild grasses, climbed a ridge, then plunged into a valley crowded with lote trees. There, he flew into a thicket of thorns, shredding his body. More and more blood began to flow. It seeped from Ukhayyad's limbs as well. His robes were ripped at the sleeves, lote thorns tearing at the light fabric up to his right shoulder. Blood flowed from shoulder to forearm. He pleaded with the crazed animal: "What do you think you're doing? Do you think you can run away from yourself? Do you think you can escape your fate? Brave men do not try to run from themselves. Wise men do not try to flee from fate. In the end, to succeed in escaping means only this: cowardice. And even if you manage to escape, it will only catch up to you one day. The jinn are your fate now. Didn't I tell you that patience is life?"

But the animal would not heed the pleading of his friend. His stomach ached terribly, and blazed with fire. *He whose foot is in the fire . . . he whose belly is on fire.*

The furious chase continued. Ukhayyad dripped with sweat, and he panted for breath. Blood poured from his arms and legs. For his part, the Mahri was drenched in a lather of sweat, pus, and blood. The fire raged in his guts and he flew through the air with increasing frenzy. A veil now covered his eyes. Reason had flown, and blindness had taken its place. Shadows descended all around, robbing him of all sense of time and matter. He was no longer conscious of whether he was galloping or standing still in the pasture. He could no longer feel his body, breath, or limbs. The pain had even consumed all sense of pain. Nothing remained but the madness in his head.

He charged through the valley of lote trees, and climbed another ridge. Unable to hold on, Ukhayyad fell to the ground.

The Mahri dragged him a short distance, then his upper lip tore away from the bridle. The camel had broken his reins. Ukhayyad rolled down the slope, the leather strap still in his hands. With effort, Ukhayyad struggled to his feet. If the camel got away from him now—at the height of his madness—Ukhayyad would never catch him again. The two would be parted forever. Had God ordained that he would say farewell to his old friend by the fall he had taken on this desolate slope? Had the time come to say goodbye forever? Ukhayyad sprang up and ran, scaling the ridge on all fours, still holding onto the reins. His lungs were splitting, his limbs tearing apart. Froth now began to appear around the young man's lips as well. Spit flew as he launched himself down the other side of the ridge. Plummeting down into the valley was his only chance. If he did not catch the camel on this slope, he would be gone forever. He marshaled everything in him that was manly, brave, and noble, he recalled all the stories of heroism he could and rushed across the slope. He flew downhill, falling, then getting back up in the blink of an eye. He fell and did not fall. In a flash, and without knowing how it happened, he found himself gripping the camel's tail. He could not believe it. Had a miracle taken place? Had he really caught the animal? Had the old stories about shame really helped? Had he triumphed over himself, over his weakness and impotence? Then it was true—it was possible to vanquish powerlessness with patience! Patience is the only talisman that can protect against the vicissitudes of fate. Patience is life itself. It was no illusion. He had just found that out. *Lord, give me a bit more patience so I can get through the rest of this journey!*

He clung to the camel's tail with his right hand. With his left, he held the reins. Weariness had sapped his strength and, despite his will to go on, his movements began to slacken. The camel yanked him and pulled him along the open desert. He found that this allowed him to catch his breath, and so he surrendered to it. He dangled from the camel's tail, his feet plowing furrows across the rich soil. They seemed to plow forever as the piebald climbed through ravines, and plunged over hills. The rocks tore away Ukhayyad's leather sandals and shredded his feet and legs. The wild plants gouged his thighs and ripped at his clothes. Ukhayyad came back to his senses and began to move his legs without letting go of the tail. With great plodding strides, the camel dragged him along.

Thirst—immortal power of the desert. Ukhayyad's throat was desiccated, his mouth parched. He tried to swallow, but failed. Yet, patience was also god of thirst. Patience, the talisman that protects forever in the desert. *God, give me patience!* When God gives you patience in the desert, he is giving you everything in the world. The pain in his hands was agonizing. Had he himself not asked for pain? Hadn't he asked God to lighten the burden of the piebald? The pain was not important. What was important was for the piebald to not escape. What was important was for the piebald to be cured. What was important was for the effect of the silphium to wear off after it had done its magic. Who knew, maybe a miracle would happen and the poor creature's health would improve. But my God, did the road to the cure have to pass through hell? Did the cure need to be accompanied by excruciating pain for it to be effective? Was the price of his mistake really so grave? Were females really such an affliction? Was the evil eye really as malevolent and lethal as this?

His right arm would soon rip out of his shoulder. And then his left arm would too. If he did nothing, he would lose his grip. What could he do? He took the reins in his left hand and used the braided leather to fasten his hand to the camel's tail. The leather was sticky and slipped out more than once. No — half solutions would not work. The knot had to be tied securely. If he could not tie it well, his hand would slip out and fall to the ground. The animal would escape and all this effort would go up in a cloud of dust. His left hand pulled on the tail and, using his right hand and his teeth, he fastened the strap around it. Gathering his remaining strength to steer the Mahri in his extraordinary gallop, Ukhayyad took comfort in the fact that he could rest as long as the strap held fast. If he succeeded in tying the reins securely, then he would also have succeeded in binding himself to the destiny of the piebald for eternity. The camel would not escape. The jinn would not steal the animal from him. He would beat the Devil himself if he had to. One more piece of patience was all he needed. One more thread.

A curtain of darkness fell.

The desert became wilder and more shadowy. Its expanse seemed to grow and grow.

A chorus of ethereal female voices trilled across the valleys from the heights of Jebel Hasawna. Their demonic ululations filled him with strength. Such calls always drive warriors on, even when they come from the throats of jinn.

His right hand went slack and he surrendered his feet. Together, man and camel plowed through the desert and obscurity.

8

Ukhayyad turned over and over in the sand, unconscious of where or who he was. He was roused only by the bright rays of the late afternoon sun. He came back to life, waking, though without waking, regaining consciousness, though not knowing who or where he was or how he got there. He lay on his stomach for some time, feeling nothing. His limbs were numb, as if they had been wrenched from his body. As he awoke, his body and head began to ache—his head as if it had been smashed open, his arms and legs as if their skin had been peeled off with a knife. He opened his eyes. Next to him, the piebald kneeled serenely in the valley, no less ragged than he. He spit blood from his mouth and looked at his body. What is this, Lord? His clothes had been torn and shredded, proving beyond a doubt that their mad course had passed through deep forested valleys. Flatland scrub would not have reached so high on a body that dangled, suspended from the tail. His body was covered with deep gashes and his body, arms, and legs were bathed in blood. Grains of sand had congealed into his wounds during the night. Sand and dirt also filled his mouth. Every now and then, he spat until he had got it all out. He tried to move his body but could not. The afternoon rays nearly blinded him. Then he looked closely at the piebald and could not believe what he saw. The poor beast was a solid red mass. He closed his eyes to rid himself of the image, then opened them again—but the vision was the same—a solid red mass. The camel had stopped bleeding, but the black skin had torn off.

He tried as hard as he could to move his limbs and crawl to the right, then used the branches of a squat broom tree to pull himself along the sand dune. His hand was still fastened to the camel's tail, preventing him from crawling any farther. He stopped what he was doing, caught his breath and went back to work until he finally was able to release the strap. Then he rolled onto his back and groaned. The pain was terrible, and continued to mount and intensify. He began to crawl again toward the camel, looking him over from the right side. A solid piece of red meat. The manged hide had fallen away during the mad journey. The piebald had shed his skin like a snake. There was not a sore to be seen. The blood had congealed across the red hide. Grains of sand clung to his belly and right side and troublesome flies treated him like a stump of freshly butchered meat.

Despite his agony, Ukhayyad was ecstatic. Would the piebald be cured? Had the miracle of silphium worked? Had the pagan shrine answered his prayers, had it responded to his pledge?

It was a miracle. A marvel.

He felt thirsty, and then remembered about water. Ukhayyad had forgotten—he was all alone in an empty waste, completely cut off from everything. The horror of his struggle with the piebald made him forget the most potent source of protection in the desert: water.

Without water, miracles cannot take place in the desert. Even when a miracle does occur, the absence of water erases it, transforming it into mere illusion. Without water, the whole world becomes a fantasy. What good is it to have your health back if you lack water? Life draws near, but so too does death. Only yesterday he had shown his readiness to sacrifice everything for his piebald to be healed. Today, just as he was seduced into hoping that a miracle might happen, the rug was pulled out from under him. It was always like that. A wholly blessed life does not exist—a thing might appear, but only to take the place of something else. Sheikh Musa used to like saying, "Perfection belongs to God alone. Carelessness blossoms with youth, but wisdom and knowledge do not take its place until the onslaught of old age and infirmity. What's the use of wisdom without youth? And what's the value of knowledge without life?"

It was always like that. Yesterday, as the piebald tried to flee his fate, at the very height of his frenzied gallop, Ukhayyad had dozed off. He slept while hanging suspended from the camel's tail. The rocks tore the skin from his feet, the bushes shredded his skin. And despite everything, despite the weariness and thirst and pain, he had slept. He did not know how or when that happened. At first, he had lost the sensation of pain. Then he lost the sensation of thirst. Then he slept as if he had passed out. If someone had told him this as a story, he wouldn't have believed that it could happen. If he had not lived through the minutiae of the fantastical event, he would never have believed it. How powerful a human being is! Ukhayyad had not known so before this moment. Yes, a human was a trivial creature—so weak and insignificant that he could be killed even by mosquitoes. At the same time he was the strongest creature in the desert, fiercer than any wild beast.

And now he had to think about how he would face the worst enemy one can have in the greater Sahara: thirst. This trial would be the greatest measure of his strength.

Ukhayyad collapsed beneath the broom tree. He filled his mouth with its twigs and began to chew them, sucking on their bitter resins. My God, how bitter the broom is! He continued to chew and their narcotic effect began to flood through him, blunting his senses and numbing his limbs—and the pain began to recede. Soon, he stood up easily, feeling light and lively. With no time to lose, he hurried to the Mahri, holding the camel's head in his arms for a few moments. The raw flesh of his neck was sticky to the touch. Poor creature. If his mate saw him like this, she would reject him forever. Just like the Devil does with humans sometimes.

Beware infection, camel—now do you see what disease can do? It can turn a creature's shape inside out! What will we do if you have lost your dappled color for good? Sheikh Musa says that perfection belongs only to God. That's right—God's blessings are never complete. There is no Garden on this earth. In this world you might enjoy your health, but beauty exists only to be lost. Perhaps it is for the best that perfection exists only for gods—if everyone was ugly, and no beauty invited the attention of the evil eye, then what malevolence could threaten us? Grotesqueness is a protection—and it offers a form of wisdom too.

Ukhayyad hugged the camel and whispered into his ear, "We've gone halfway. Now we'll go the remaining distance, the part that'll be the hardest for me. All my water spilled out during our mad journey. Now you must save me. We'll head for the nearest well in the lower valleys. Do not attempt to carry me to the oases. I'll die before we get very far along that road. There's not a single drop of water in me, I can't store water like you. Do you understand? You do not want to lose your old friend, your new brother. Now—there's no time to lose."

He looked for the reins and staggered dizzily, nearly falling to the ground. He clung to the Mahri's neck and dug in the sand under his belly. There, he placed one end of the reins. He went to the other side of the camel and pulled on the leather strap. He pulled himself up to sit behind the Mahri's hump and tied the reins around his waist. The position was not a comfortable one. He stretched out over the camel's back, gluing himself to the wet flesh. The red flesh was sticky to his touch, the blood not yet dry. Ukhayyad's body, now also naked, fused with the viscous flesh of the Mahri. Flesh met flesh, blood mixed with blood. In the past they had been merely friends. Today, they had been joined by a much stronger tie. Those who become brothers by sharing blood are closer than those who share parentage. A mother might give birth to two boys without their ever becoming brothers. As long as their blood does not mingle, they can never share this deeper bond. Becoming someone's brother is easier said than done.

He cinched the cord around his body and secured it to the back of the Mahri. Ukhayyad kicked him lightly, and the Mahri rose to his feet. He stood motionless for a moment, then began to move. He did not retrace the way they came, but headed south instead. They first passed through a valley, then climbed a ridge. There, camel and rider were swallowed up by the endless flatlands. Ukhayyad's eyes melted into the limitless horizon. The camel walked on, with wide, firm steps—the steps of one ready to cross waterless wastes.

It was midday, and ghosts danced before Ukhayyad's eyes. Soon, he faded back into the shadows.

9

With the first fall, Ukhayyad found himself perched between consciousness and oblivion, in that interval between life and death. Using his teeth, he re-attached his hand to the tail so quickly that he never left his semi-conscious state. Being in this no man's land between heaven and hell inspired him to return to the trick he had used before. He tumbled and got back up over and over. He fell into a daze and, parched, licked at the urine when it trickled down the camel's thigh. It had been divine inspiration to tie his hand to the camel's tail.

He imagined that the camel was descending from a tall mountain. At that point, he transcended all bounds of consciousness and crossed over again into the shadows.

Returning from his brutal journey into half-conscious oblivion, Ukhayyad found himself atop the well at Awal. He groped around its stony lip for a bucket, but found none. With his teeth, he untied his hand from the camel. The strap had carved a deep gash around his wrist, and now he wore a bracelet of blood. He felt no pain, nothing but sticky fluid. He licked his hand, but tasted nothing. Things were covered in a haze of fog and shadow.

His eyes had lost their ability to see a long time ago, perhaps because he had lingered so long in that interval between this world and the hereafter. But life's force stirred his dead limbs, filling them with an unvanquished will to continue moving.

Ukhayyad now fastened the leather reins to his ankle. He tied the knot securely and examined the place where the strap joined the tail. He stumbled, stupefied, trying to locate the Mahri's neck, then head. He wanted to tell the camel something before he plunged into the bottomless well. He never doubted whether he would return. At that peculiar moment, he thought about what Sheikh Musa said about death: it was closer than your jugular vein and yet farther than the ends of the earth. He wanted to tell the piebald this. He wanted to tell him what to do as he plunged into the abyss. The piebald lavished the young man with attention, covering him with his lips and licking his face. Ukhayyad was unable to see the other's eyes and unable to utter a word. He had lost the ability to speak. First he had lost his sight, and now he had lost his voice. He raised his right hand and patted the Mahri's head. Man and camel spoke to one another, as brothers, by way of gesture. His head began to spin and he looked for the mouth of the well. He stepped out, over the lip, his unfettered leg dangling over the pit. The thought of death never occurred to him. He thought only about what he would say to Sheikh Musa, "Death truly lies closer than your jugular vein, and yet, it is still very difficult for a man to die. Death lies beyond the furthest end of the world. When you arrive at a well, of course there will be no pail. Or you might find a pail, but don't then expect to find the well that goes with it. It's always like that." He held onto the stones that lined the lip of the well. Then he began to crawl into the hole. He saw nothing, heard nothing, and felt nothing. He struggled, using his hands to clamber down the first rows of stone and hoping to avoid a free fall that would yank the strap from the camel's tail. His descent was automatic, unconscious. He lowered himself into the rock, until his strength—the limbs that had been smashed by journey and injury—betrayed him and he fell into the abyss.

An entire lifetime passed in the fraction of a second that came between the stone lip of the well and the water below. An eon went by, taking him back, beyond the day he was born. During that moment, he saw his own birth pass before his eyes. He saw himself as he fell from his mother's womb into the chasm. He heard the trilling of she-jinn on Jebel Hasawna. He saw the shadows of houris in paradise. It was one of these dark-eyed virgins wearing a diaphanous mantle who then caught him and gently placed him down into heaven's river. Here, in this river of paradise, he began to drink.

Then he began to choke and gag. He did not vomit in the well itself, but outside. If he could have opened his eyes, he would have seen a vision of the piebald, and the rays of the sun, glaring sharply like fiery spurs. The piebald had carried out his unspoken command—he had pulled him out of that freshwater sea.

Once more he returned to the space between, and ascended, one more time, into the world of shadows.

10

When the herders brought their camels to the well, they found the young man's emaciated, bloody body stretched out naked beneath its edge. His foot was still fastened to the tail of a thoroughbred Mahri that looked as if he had been skinned alive. The camel stood over his head, using his body to shield him from the scorching sun. They carried him into the shade of a nearby lote tree. Under that thick canopy crown, they dunked his head into a bucket and poured water over him. An old herder hastened to light a fire and heat a kettle of water. The man rifled through his belongings and returned with a handful of fenugreek seeds that he proceeded to cook. The camel herder served the broth to him with a spoon, all the while holding his head like mothers do when they breast-feed their children.

A few days later, Ukhayyad began to talk. He spoke to the old man about the piebald, "Did you know he was a piebald? Have you ever seen a piebald Mahri in the desert? Don't pay any attention to his condition right now—it's just a passing sickness. His original colors will come back. They have to come back."

The herders exchanged looks among themselves. The old herder watched him with intense curiosity, then smiled a benign smile. The smile of one who has seen much in the world.

Ukhayyad asked abruptly, "Do you think he's lost his original color?"

The old man said, while pouring tea from one pot to another, "Lord only knows. The Sufi sheikhs of Ghadamès say that everything returns to its original form in the end. The seedling grows into the broom tree. The broom tree blossoms. Its flowers turn to fruit. Fruit brings forth seeds which fall to the ground. If his original form was piebald, then that color will return to his form in time. Be patient, and do not fear."

Then he smiled again.

"If his colors don't return, his health will have no meaning," Ukhayyad replied, impatiently. "His cure has already cost us so much."

"Would you have preferred to purchase his health without suffering?"

"Without his dappled color, he has no health." His fear that the Mahri might have lost his original color for good stuck in his throat. He forgot the sweet taste of health and rescue from death. The herders clothed him and gave him a veil and supplies. They escorted him as far as the end of the Hamada desert. There, they bid him farewell and returned to the lower valleys where they made their camps.

Shame prevented Ukhayyad from bringing the piebald into the camp while he was in this state. Using a cord the herders had given him, Ukhayyad tethered him in a pasture just north of the plain where his kin's encampments stretched far and wide.

Of all his belongings, nothing remained but the reins. He coiled them around his wrist, determined to preserve them as a memento of his journey. They consisted of a polished strap, painstakingly braided and branded with geometric designs that had faded from long use. That thin leather strap had been the sole material connecting him to life, the cord that took him from his purgatory, where he hovered in the shadows, and delivered him back to the desert again. It was the thread that had bound him to the piebald during that first mad journey and had joined their destinies. It had held him again during his second journey that stretched between the mouth of the well to the surface of the waters. These reins marked that distance between one reality and the other. They embodied the threshold where he had heard the howls of the she-jinn of Jebel Hasawna and where he had seen the houris of paradise. In these reins was distilled the moment in which he was given drink from heaven's stream. In them was also an eon that measured the whole of his life in the desert. The reins marked the moment when he tumbled headlong into an abyss, lighting his soul with a dark flame that would never go out. Without this thread connecting one extreme and the other, that mystical moment would never have come into being. Without this thread, he would never have seen that mysterious spark whose kernel he was unable to divulge, even to himself. Is this spark what wine drinkers see in their moment of abandon? Is it what the Sufi sheikhs of the Tijaniya brotherhood referred to when they spoke of their encounter with God? He had seen dervishes in the Adrar oasis, spinning wildly when suddenly one of them flew into ecstasy. The man had pulled out his knife and plunged it into his chest, expecting to complete the journey back to God, hoping to savor an encounter with the infinite. Sheikhs, like Sheikh Musa of the Qadiriya sect, accused the Tijanis of heresy and fought them wherever they met. War broke out from time to time between adherents of the two sects. The hostilities had even reached far into the desert wilderness itself, carried to the distant pastures by wandering dervishes and itinerant travelers who accompanied the long-distance caravans. Had he seen a vision of this magnificent fate in that flash of a moment?

The sheikh visited him in the tent Ukhayyad's father had erected specially for receiving the visitors and well-wishers who came to congratulate him on his safe return from the vast, labyrinthine desert. The sheikh said, "A beautiful thing can be bought only at great price. And health is the most beautiful thing in this world. So, have no regrets about what you have been through."

At nightfall, the two went off alone into the open desert. "Did you suffer much?" The sheikh asked, seeking to comfort him.

Ukhayyad did not answer. Something else was worrying him. Impatient, he asked, "Will the piebald go back to his original state?"

The sheikh asked him to explain with a nod of his head. The young man asked more bluntly, "Will his color return?"

"God is beautiful and He loves beauty and camels," Musa smiled in the twilight. "You've paid for his cure with much suffering. If it is perfection you want, then you will have to pay for that as well."

Ukhayyad did not understand. The sheikh clarified, "Think about it. He needs to be cleansed."

"Cleansed?"

"Purified—he needs to be gelded."

"Gelded?"

"What else? Didn't we agree that everything has its price?"

". . ."

"His whole body carries the mark of sin. His body is an offense in itself. We need to remove the cause at the root."

The young man stood silent. "I cannot come to this decision by myself," he eventually said. "I need to consult with others. I have to think about it some."

Then Ukhayyad turned and disappeared into the darkness.

II

The harm you've caused us was enough," Ukhayyad said when he and the camel were off by themselves again in the pasture. "Women cause nothing but headaches, don't they?" By now, the camel's new skin had toughened, and his wounds had mended. The ghastly redness had disappeared. But the camel's coat had yet to grow back. When the Mahri did not comment on his proposition, the young men continued: "Sheikh Musa says the root cause must be removed. Splendor is no easy thing to attain, everything demands its own sacrifice. You won't be in pain for long. We will do it during the summer. Summer is the best season for it."

Agitated, the piebald reared his head. Was this his way of showing that he rejected the idea? "No, no—wait," Ukhayyad blurted out. "Don't rush into decisions that you'll later regret. What happened to you should never have happened. Warriors have no business contracting contagious skin diseases. Purebreds should not allow themselves to get mange. Have you seen any other piebald with mange? You're a splendid creature, you're beautiful. But beauty can't be bought with mere money. For your looks, I am ready to pay with my life. To be the most beautiful thoroughbred in the Sahara—you have no idea what that would be like. Do you think I would ever do something that would cause you harm? Do you have so little trust in me?"

The piebald opened his jaws as wide as they would go. The outlines of a wicked laugh twinkled in his keen eyes. "I get it," Ukhayyad also laughed. "You mean to say that females are more beautiful still! No—don't lie, by God! Women are beautiful, yes. Even lovely. But so are snakes. And like snakes, they bite. You've been bitten by one, and look what her venom did to you the last time. Wasn't that enough? Have some shame—turn your back on the ways of the Devil!"

He stroked the Mahri's neck and inspected his hide, whispering, "When we get through this ordeal, we'll begin something new. We'll learn how to dance. Purebred camels must know how to dance, and you have never tried. It'll make you forget all about love. Trust me. You'll soar through the air, and sail through the heavens. It's more dignified to see God in heaven, isn't it, than to chase after silly she-camels on earth?"

He sat in front of the camel in the open desert, his hands wrapped around his knees. "There's no way around it," he said. "Without purification, you will never attain beauty and never meet God. Without purity, nothing. I admit it is a nasty business, but we have no other choice."

Then summer arrived and with it came time to perform all manner of work. Ukhayyad disappeared, using the pretext of traveling to the oasis of Gariyat to retrieve camels that had strayed there. He left the piebald in the hands of executioners. Only Sheikh Musa was aware that Ukhayyad had left, not to chase after camels, but to flee from the appointed day.

The day after he departed, the men gathered around the poor camel. They spent the morning struggling to remove the scourge from his body. They spent the afternoon, in accordance with custom, making the camel swallow his own testicles.

When Ukhayyad returned from his journey, he found the Mahri anxious. He stroked the animal's body and massaged the mended skin. The piebald's eyes were swollen with sadness. He led the camel into the southern pastures where they could be alone. Ukhayyad took some barley out of his sack and held the grain in his hands. The camel turned away. Ukhayyad followed after him with the food, but the animal stubbornly refused his advances. "I know why you're so rough with me," Ukhayyad said, returning the grain to his knapsack. "You're angry because I left you and went off. I did not abandon you. We had agreed to it together. We've guaranteed the return of your color. Now, you'll return to being a piebald like before. Aren't you looking forward to seeing yourself dappled, beautiful, and rare?"

The piebald's eyes welled up with tears and Ukhayyad hugged him. They stood a while embracing in the infinite expanse just as the night began to thicken.

The gods do not forgive those who break promises.

Sophocles

12

But the piebald had not forgiven him. The humiliation in the dancing arena was a sign that he had not. Had Ukhayyad misjudged things? Camels do not forget wrongs. They are like slaves — and you had better watch out if you mistreat them.

Instead of celebrating him, that damned poetess had composed a nasty ode skewering the camel. "His color is spotted, but his mind is rotted," was how it began. Within two days, echoes of the poem had traveled throughout the entire encampment. He would cut out that wretched woman's tongue and give her a taste of his whip.

One day soon after the dance fiasco, he took the purebred to the pasture. There, away from everything else, Ukhayyad scolded him. He made the camel kneel under the lote tree and began to shout, gesturing into the air with his whip: "What did I do to you to deserve this from you? You should be thanking me, not trying to humiliate me. Just look at your colors — you're even more dappled than before. If I hadn't rescued you, your splendor would have disappeared altogether."

The Mahri protested, turning his head askance, but Ukhayyad blocked him. "Don't try to get away," he yelled angrily. "We're settling our accounts today. Didn't you hear the poem that wicked poetess composed about you? She has been watching us for a long time, waiting for us to make a mistake. I commissioned her to sing your praises, and she insisted on seeing you dance before she did. Then you decided to spite me during the dance—and see what happened? She composed a poem ridiculing us instead! Are you happy now?"

He rose to his feet, clapped his hands as if to say "I'm done," and wandered across the open desert space, kicking away rocks with his sandals. "I'm so stupid. So stupid," he repeated. "Instead of paying our debt as quickly as possible, we argue and fight. We need to make good on the promise we made. Have you forgotten the pledge we made?" But it was Ukhayyad, and not the Mahri, who had forgotten their promise.

Still, Ukhayyad had not altogether forgotten that he had pledged to sacrifice a camel at the shrine. In fact, he had purchased a purebred camel from a sheikh who was emigrating to Mecca. Ukhayyad traded a splendid Touat kilim rug for the animal. The sheikh had come from Marrakesh, saying that he had decided to leave this world behind. He said he wanted to spend the rest of his days in Mecca where he might live near the Prophet's grave. The tribe slaughtered a goat for the man and feted him for three days. He cast off the rest of his possessions and sold off the last of his animals. The camel had been given as a gift to Ukhayyad, the ascetic sheikh insisted. He had not bartered the camel for the rug, he said, but had accepted it because he needed a prayer rug.

Ukhayyad recalled the promise he uttered at the tomb of the ancients: "O lord of the desert, god of the ancients, I pledge to bring you a fat camel, sound of body and mind." But that camel was not yet fat, nor yet of sound mind and body. Ukhayyad decided to wait for the animal to mature and fatten. At the time of his humiliation in the dance arena, the young purebred was still grazing hungrily in the southern pastures. Ukhayyad recognized that what had taken place was a sign of something. The lord of the desert was announcing his presence and warning him—he was demanding that the offering should not be delayed any longer.

Thereafter, other events occurred. Fate brought with it carelessness, and Ukhayyad's life took another course. There was nothing strange about this turn at all. Like prophecies, signs flicker into view only for one moment before they disappear and are gone forever.

13

"Marry her and be damned."

This was the message Ukhayyad's father sent him through Sheikh Musa. He had not expected this sort of response, and it filled his eyes with a cloud of rage. Sheikh Musa tried to warn him. "Gently," he said as he shook his finger. "Fathers may speak to sons however they like, but a son cannot answer his father in kind." Ukhayyad swallowed his anger and rose to hide his humiliation in the desert.

The reason for all this was that an Eve had joined the tribe to help herd the skinny she-goats. The gorgeous girl came with her kin from Aïr, fleeing the drought that had gripped that part of the desert over the last five years. While unmistakable signs of affliction showed on the miserable beasts of her tribe, her beauty remained in full bloom. Not even the dusty road had stripped her of her splendor. Besides her beauty, she had a light spirit and a great deal of charm. It was this charm that slew Ukhayyad the first time they met.

Beware the charms of women! Their allure is a mystery—it is as plain and simple as the desert itself and yet there is nothing more obscure or indecipherable. Their charm is like the murmuring of jinn on Jebel Hasawna—you hear it, but cannot make out the words, or you hear the sounds, but their meaning escapes you. A look might suggest a woman's charm—or an offhand smile, passing glance, shake of the head, or the way a word is spoken. Or it might be nothing more than a musical ring in her voice. The allure of women was something created just to slay men like Ukhayyad.

He first met her during a moonlit gathering. He watched her bewitching smile flash in the dim light and followed her slim silhouette as she wandered between the women. Then he heard her sing. My God—what a powerful voice! Her songs welled up from deep inside. She sang as if she were plucking out the loneliness from her heart. She sang as if she were exorcising the bleak solitude of the desert. Her divine voice communicated what her charms could never directly express. Each man who heard her sing that night began to swoon and dance. Ukhayyad danced with the other young men until morning.

He met her in passing after that, both during the late-night gatherings and in the pastures. She would sing heavenly songs for him out in the open desert spaces and he would listen attentively to the agony of a girl who had been driven by drought and famine to emigrate and live in exile from her homeland. It was not difficult to find this melody among the people of the desert. Who in the desert had never tasted drought? Who had not been driven into exile by famine? Such things were the inescapable fate of the desert—and all the songs of the desert were an expression of this grief, drought, and homelessness. The peoples of the desert sang of endless exile, of the eternal longing to return to God's presence and the origin of all. They sang of longing for that ever-merciful oasis, the original oasis, the oasis of which the oases of Fezzan were but miserable ghosts. The oasis that no longer exists, that never existed.

Ukhayyad had caught a glimpse of that oasis when he tumbled into the well. But now that mystery had vanished. Now it was the girl's songs of longing and agony that made him burn—and in his heart, he wept. He spoke with the girl often, asking about Aïr, the drought, and the grief of emigrating from Timbuktu. Then they played, reciting lines of poetry back and forth to one another. She knew more poems by heart than she had hairs on her head. Her hair was itself a poem of braided plaits falling thickly across a full bosom.

He went to her uncle to ask for her hand, and won his approval. He then sent word to his father, asking for his counsel, and was stunned by the response, "Marry her and be damned!" He did not understand his father at all—he had never lived with the man and did not know him well. All he knew was that women held first place in his father's life. His mother had occupied second rank among his wives. The poor woman was sickly and weak in body and heart. Ukhayyad remembered her colorless face right before she died. Her heart killed her before Ukhayyad's seventh birthday. An African slave woman had raised him after that. Ukhayyad's father then married another woman from the clans of the vassals. He married her before he became chief, but they never produced any offspring. Even with all these wives, the man's adventures with other women had never ceased throughout the years. He was famous for often repeating the saying of the Prophet, "The three dearest things to me in your world are: women, perfume, and—most of all—prayer." He then liked to offer his commentary, "See? Women come first. They're at the top of the Prophet's list." When the clan engaged in raids into the African interior, his father would relinquish his share of the spoils save for what he was owed of the women captives. He would then snatch them up, carrying them back into the desert as his concubines. He had even married a number of them according to God's law, despite the fact that they were heathens who knew nothing of Islam. In the clan, it was said that back when Ukhayyad was a small child, his parents had fallen out because of how the man carried on with a beautiful mulatta who lived in a neighboring encampment. After Ukhayyad's mother passed away, his father became chief, inheriting the title from his maternal uncle who had died unexpectedly. It was said that the uncle had not intended to leave the leadership to Ukhayyad's father, but had died precipitously, ambushed by bandits in the Danbaba desert, and the sheikhs of the clan had not been able to go against custom simply because of the nephew's well-known passion for women. In those days, a passion for women was not seen as a vice that compromised a man's virility. On the contrary, to be passionate, even mad for a woman was a virtue thought to befit warriors and noblemen. Ukhayyad's father bolstered his standing by repeating the lofty saying of the Prophet concerning women. In doing so, he effectively ambushed and neutralized the men of religion, ensuring his immunity from the malicious interference of would-be religious scholars and people who think that Islamic law should be used to settle disputes.

Like his father before him, Ukhayyad also learned a few Qur'anic verses from a blind sheikh who spent his life wandering with the clan. Then the sheikh died from the bubonic plague, and his place was taken by Sheikh Musa, who not only educated him, but also treated him like a sincere friend. Noticing the coolness of the youth's relationship with his father, Sheikh Musa took an interest in Ukhayyad and helped to ease the early loss of his mother. Despite the introverted character Ukhayyad had inherited from his mother, the sheikh found a path to his heart. The first time was when he rescued the boy from the flashflood. That day, some people of the tribe thought they heard thunder echoing through the mountains to the north. But others told them they were wrong, writing off the possibility of such a miraculous thing. "Who's ever seen rain in the desert in the middle of the summer? When have the southern winds ever brought a downpour?" They said that those who sounded the alarm had heard nothing more than the call of Resurrection Day—and they ridiculed the idea that a roar of thunder had been heard by anybody. And so, no one bothered to move out of the low-lying valley. At night's end, when the deluge came, it swept away the entire tribe. The only one who clearly foresaw the flashflood that night was Sheikh Musa. When the torrent surprised the encampment, he was squatting, reciting his devotionals in front of his tent.

The young Ukhayyad had been sleeping under the moonlight in the tent door, while his old African slave took refuge from snakes and wolves by sleeping further inside. In a dream, he watched as glowing embers floated, unextinguished, across a large body of water. Then he was swimming beside the hot embers as they began to die. Dream mixed with reality as he awoke from his sleep. All was chaos—the old woman was shrieking, along with the other women and children in the camp. Men shouted and goats bellowed. The roar of the water shook the earth, but even all this could not drown out the soft hissing sound of embers as they died in the waters of his dream. That hissing sound would reverberate in his ears forever.

Sheikh Musa swooped by, snatching the old woman with his right hand, and clasping the boy to his waist with his left. He raced them across the valley. The only thing Ukhayyad remembered from that experience was the faint whisper, the soft hissing of the embers.

14

heikh Musa had mediated between father and son during their first falling out. At that time, Ukhayyad's father had wanted his sons to inherit the title of chief, to keep it from falling into the hands of outsiders. The man was determined to marry his son to his sister's daughter. The girl was sister to a nephew, Mukhammed, who was preparing to take over as chief. In a message Musa delivered to Ukhayyad, the father emphasized that this was their one chance to secure the title within their household. For if his sister's daughter married Ukhayyad and they produced a boy, then the family's honor would be guaranteed. It never occurred to Ukhayyad to think of Mukhammed's sister. She was a dim-witted girl with dull eyes, lacking all spark and poetry — she was an ordinary, even sickly girl without charm or talent. To him, there was nothing womanly about her, nothing feminine — so how then could he marry her? He cursed the idea of becoming chief, and sent a message to his father: he would not do it. The man never said a word about his son's rudeness until now. Today, he had replied to Ukhayyad's earlier insult in kind: "Marry her and be damned." The message burned Ukhayyad to the core.

He did not need Sheikh Musa to remind him of the significance of this message. Every young man in the desert knew that heaven opened its doors each morning to receive the prayers of fathers.

Ukhayyad had inherited his father's obstinacy, but not the man's desire to lead the tribe. He had taken up the man's tenacious nature, but not his love for status among men—and stubbornness was far more useful in the struggles against the desert. From his perspective, being chief brought nothing but headache. He who has visited the houris of paradise and who has drunk from heaven's river would never seek to inherit the title of chief!

So he made up his mind and chose Ayur. He fled the throne and plunged into the embrace of a goddess of charm and allure. He married the young refugee and repeated the very mantra his father had taken from the Prophet: "The dearest things to me in your world are three: women, perfume, and—most of all—prayer."

He chose woman. But, in time, this same woman would be the one to bring about the piebald's ruin. And the camel Ukhayyad had pledged to the saint so long ago, the camel he had left to fatten up in the pastures, would be the same camel he slaughtered instead for the feast on his wedding night.

15

So it was that his father disowned him. The man told Sheikh Musa, "Tell that idiot son of mine that the Tuareg are smart to pass things down on the mother's side. Tell him to take his girl and go back to the land of sorcerers—go back to Kano and Timbuktu!"

When his father cut him off from his inheritance, Ukhayyad left the tribe. But he did not head for Aïr, the land of sorcerers— the drought there had been driving more and more refugees toward the northern Sahara. Instead, he departed toward the lower valleys that lay on the outskirts of the Fezzan oases. There he wandered during the rainy months alongside migrants from many tribes and nations. During the dry summer months, he settled in the oases until his first son was born.

At that time, foreign invaders finally broke the resistance along the coasts and began pouring across the northern desert. The area of the red Hamada desert had witnessed many bloody events. Emissaries arrived, looking to gather fighters. Ukhayyad went off with the piebald to talk in private. "What did you think—that life was one long melody?" he asked. "You need to understand: men do not have the privilege of calling themselves warriors until they have gone to war and come back. You're not a true nobleman if you have not tasted battle. This is our chance."

But this is not what fate had in store for them. News came that the resistance in the Hamada had been crushed, and that his father had died a martyr during the fighting. It was said he fought bravely. In fact, people throughout the desert composed odes afterwards, glorifying his courage. Perhaps they did this because they were not expecting a man who was a perennial marrier of wives—and moreover a slave to his passion for kidnapped African girls—to record such glorious deeds in fighting the Italians. One of the herders told Ukhayyad that his father had kept his head, even during a blitz attack on them. He went around the tribe recruiting fighters and fought until his camp was surrounded. The siege went on until a disagreement erupted among them. Some of the sheikhs had been broken by thirst, and thought they had all better surrender. Ukhayyad's father and a number of loyal men went off by themselves to make their final stand on Jebel Hasawna. There, he had died of thirst. At that point, the tribe surrendered, as had many other tribes. After a long interval, Ukhayyad's cousin became sheikh, but there was nothing in that fact for the man to enjoy, since the tribe had been scattered to the four corners of the earth. Some of the families took refuge in Ghadamès, others in Tamanresset. Others still resolved to emigrate to the Sudan. The new sheikh's mission to reunite them came to nothing. He had failed to convince the other sheikhs to wait patiently for the calamity to pass, and was wandering about the deserts still, seeking to regather the families under his leadership. If only the tribes in the wide desert would disband completely—then power disputes would vanish, and brother would no longer have to fight brother.

At precisely that time, a relative of Ukhayyad's wife came to stay with them as a guest. From the south, he had come with a caravan laden with gold, ivory, and ostrich feathers, all of which he had managed to sell in Ghadamès before it was over-run by the flood of invaders. With the money, he purchased herds of camels, and took up with a group of herders in the Danbaba desert.

Having remained there for a number of months, he placed the camels in the care of the other men. He then came to visit Ukhayyad and his wife in their summer quarters in the Adrar oasis. Dudu, as he was called, told Ukhayyad that Ayur was related to him on his mother's side and that he would come to check on her as one of his kin. Ukhayyad recognized a familiar tenacity in the man's eyes—the brutal resolve of those forced to migrate forever, a determination that concealed secrets no tongue could utter.

During the man's stay, Ukhayyad could not restrain himself. It was not long before he divulged the extent of his attachment to the piebald camel. He sang his list of questions to the stranger: "Have you ever seen a piebald Mahri in the desert before?"; "Have you ever seen a camel with such grace, light-ness, and stature?"; "Have you ever seen anything more beautiful and dignified?" The guest would smile between every question and the next, shaking his head. "No." Inexperienced, Ukhayyad did not know that idle talk leads one to reveal secrets. And according to the law of the desert, divulging secrets to strangers can cost a refugee his life—or so say the fortunetellers, who have it on the authority of the witch doctors and soothsayers in Kano.

Dudu lodged with them in the oasis for a number of days and then asked their leave to travel. He sold a pair of camels to some peasants to supply himself with dates and barley. Then he returned to his camel herd, promising to visit them again when circumstances permitted. After the guest had left, Ukhayyad discovered that the man had left him a surprise; he had hidden a sack of dates and a sack of barley in Ukhayyad's underground cache.

16

wo days later, the sacks were stolen from the cache. In the sand above where they had been stored, a sign had been left for him by the thief—the clear outline of a triangle traced in dry dates. The shape puzzled Ukhayyad and he asked the blind old woman from Tiba to read its hidden meaning. The soothsayer asked, "You said it was a triangle? Did you ever promise something to the goddess Tanit?"

His head split, and he leaped like someone who had been stabbed. "Tanit?" He remembered his pledge. He recollected the saint and the pyramid-shaped tomb. But he had eaten the animal and fed the offering to his bride. He had completely forgotten about his earlier promise. Was this a sign from Tanit? That was her mark. It was the same shape that was branded on the forearms of men and tattooed on the women's abdomens. In the darkness of night, he had even seen it on Ayur's belly. The same design was carved into sword handles and engraved on leather saddle horns and satchels. It was etched into gun barrels and embroidered into clothes. Tanit's mark appeared everywhere and on everything. Was the disappearance of the two bags a cautionary reminder? Have mercy, Tanit! I did forget—I failed to recognize your sign on the pyramid pedestal! In my weakness, I neglected my promise!

After war broke out along the northern coasts, the movement of caravans through the interior of the continent began to falter, then stopped. The famine intensified and spread across the entire desert. At first, this did not affect desert commerce. But as the war went on, it drove peasants to raise the price on grains and dates. Later, many began to bury their harvests in secret caches, and refused to barter or buy. Those two sacks had disappeared at the very moment Ukhayyad had needed them the most. That only increased his rage and self-loathing. And his contempt for women.

He despised women because, now, he looked at things with his eyes rather than his heart; and as his feelings melted into cool reason, Ayur's magic began to dissipate. He had once thought that her charm would last forever. Once upon a time, he had thought it was as powerful as the vision of fate he saw during his tumble into the well. Now, he was certain that to draw near to love was to bury oneself in a grave. Now he knew that the passing of time was a kind of magical charm as well, one that broke love's spell and scattered its poetry.

It was this woman who had brought calamity on the piebald; she had driven Ukhayyad to break his promise. He had never before broken an oath in his life. Now, without thinking, he had done so. And with whom? With the hieroglyphs of the ancients, with the goddess Tanit herself. He wished he had known it was her shrine, or he would not have forgotten. But truth only shows itself after time has passed. This is the law of truth, on the authority of the elders who repeat it over and over.

He concealed his secret from the soothsayer and stepped out into the open desert. He sat until midnight, unable to arrive at a solution to his problem. Since he had realized the truth only after the fact, and only after famine had come to reign in the desert, there was no way to fight fate's prescription. Where would he find a healthy, strong, and sane camel after these lean, dry years? How would he acquire a camel when he himself went without food and when his wife and child were nearly starving? He recalled an incident in a sandy region of the desert a few weeks earlier when he had cooked his leather sandal and eaten it. Ukhayyad had been following the tracks of a camel he had purchased back in easier times and then left to pasture in a valley between the northern and southern deserts. Along the way, he met one of the herders there who told him that he had seen the camel weeks before toward the east. He rode on the back of the piebald until he arrived at Zurzatin, and the herders of the Kel Abada there told him that they had seen thieves taking the animal with a herd of stolen camels across the eastern desert toward Ghadamès where they would be sold. Their stories contradicted one another and did not make sense. Others claimed that bandits had slaughtered and eaten the camel right where they found him. In a daze, Ukhayyad wandered about, hungry and miserable. He had not tasted real food in days. Despite that, he refused the invitation of the Kel Abada to eat with them. The sandy parts of the desert promised nothing. They were treacherous and devoid of herbs, scrub brush, and game. The desert of the Hamada was paradise compared to this heartless place. In the Hamada, if you did not find a gazelle or moufflon, it would offer you a rabbit. If you did not find a rabbit, it would give you a lizard. If it was not the right season for reptiles, the Hamada would set you a green table garnished with wild herbs. If the heavens held back their rains, the Hamada would show you mercy, providing you with the fruits of the lote tree left over from the previous year. My God—how merciful the Hamada was! In contrast, this desert fed you nothing but sand, dust, and the scorching southern winds.

When he could stand it no longer, he took off his leather sandal. He gathered wood and lit a fire. He roasted the leather on the fire until it became soft and puckered—then he devoured it. It was delicious, not any different from the camel skins he had eaten many times before. He opened his eyes after the meal. He began to stare at the piebald's profile. It seemed to him that the camel was smirking. His eyes were smiling, laughing at him. He stood up and shook his finger at him, warning, "You better not tell anyone what you saw here. Do you understand? This is my secret."

He removed the other sandal and studied it in his hands. Collapsing on the ground, he spoke to his friend as if he were addressing himself: "Don't laugh at me. A warrior is also a pitiful creature—someone who might eat his sandal when he's dying of hunger. Don't measure me by your standards. Unlike you, God didn't give me a place to store water and food. Hunger strikes down even the noblest of creatures. Starvation can bring even sultans to their knees and force them to grovel like slaves. Show some mercy!"

I heard Sufyan ibn Ainiya once say, "Those with children never have enough and never find rest. We used to have a cat that never once got into our cooking pots. But as soon as she gave birth to kittens, she started to."

Cited in *The Great Book of Asceticism*
by the Imam Abu Bakr Ahmad ibn Husayn al-Bayhaqi

17

Ukhayyad woke up in the night, alarmed.

He had seen the local soothsayer standing over him, telling him to slaughter the piebald.

He wiped away the sweat and slipped out of the hut. A pale moon peeked timidly in the sky. In the magnificent silence of the oasis, the night-time singing of crickets could be heard in the palm grove. He walked about the open desert and thought: this soothsayer from Tiba must be a ghoul. What he had seen was not a real dream, but a ghost who wanted to eat the piebald's flesh. Who would dare to eat the flesh of a stately animal with graceful limbs?

Tomorrow he would find the witch and kill her in cold blood. But, beforehand, he would find out what she meant by telling him this. Perhaps that too had been a sign of something else. The language of soothsayers is never self-evident. He returned to the hut, but was afraid to go back to sleep. Those who suffer nightmares fear the bed.

In the morning, a peasant woman told him that the soothsayer from Tiba had left the oasis. Her son had come and taken her away with him in a caravan passing toward Aghadès. Three days after the woman had left, Ukhayyad saw her in a dream. She spoke to him directly: "I am not the one who demands the head of your piebald. It is Tanit." Then she vanished, and he never saw her again after that. In a few days, he forgot her altogether. He returned to his old self and devoted his energies to staving off the hunger that surrounded them. Only the day before, a whole family—husband, wife, and three children—had died. The doors of life had closed in their face and they shut themselves up in a hut. No one saw them until their corpses began to rot and one of their neighbors broke down the door. They found the family heaped in a pile, their bodies decomposed and crawling with maggots. The children's eyes had almost popped out of their sockets. The imam at the mosque said that they had been strangled to death. Apparently, the father had choked them to prevent neighbors from hearing their cries.

That night, Ayur told him, "If you don't do something about the state we're in, we might as well do what that family did. But we should do it out in the desert rather than here. There will always be three bullets for your rifle, right?"

He did not reply.

In the morning, he went to the merchant to borrow some oil. He had known the man during better times and had bartered with him in the past, exchanging strips of dried gazelle and moufflon meat for barley, dates, and sugar. The man would not turn him away disappointed. But the merchant swore that he did not have enough for his own supper. He did not have enough for his own supper?! Only a few months ago the man had received a caravan from Timbuktu and purchased their entire merchandise. Then he turned around and quickly sold the same goods at twice the price to the merchants of Ghadamès. Then, as the food shortage intensified, he began to sell them at exorbitant prices to the peasants. Once a profiteer, always a profiteer! The merchant had caught the whiff of starvation before it had started to spread. He knew the war would go on and on.

Ukhayyad remembered his wife's ambiguous hint, and the hidden hatred it concealed. A woman despises nothing as much as she despises a failure or a man convinced that he is a failure. Toward such a man, she can be openly hostile, even if he is her most intimate relation. How brutal woman can be! My God— where had her charms gone? Where was her poetry, her spark? He asked one of the peasants for food, but the man swore the same thing. When times get tough, all men make oaths and then break them. The peasants were terrified of the future, of the unknown, of the surprises war would bring.

Ukhayyad sat for a long time on the edge of the water channel. Then he got up to leave. But he had only gone a short distance when the peasant caught up to him. Tears glimmered in the man's eyes. He opened his hands to reveal a few dry dates. Three, maybe four dates. The man said, "These are from my children. They are for your child. I know you have a boy."

The man raised his face and completed the gesture by addressing his words toward heaven: "Lord, what sins have these children committed?"

Ukhayyad studied the four dates for a few moments. Tears welled in his eyes too. He hid them with his veil and hid the dates in his pocket. Before disappearing into the date grove, Ukhayyad heard the peasant cry out, "Why don't you sell the Mahri? Why should a man like you starve when he owns a Mahri like yours?"

Ukhayyad froze. How dare he? Did the ignorant man suppose the piebald was merely a beast? Would he have Ukhayyad eat the flesh of his brother? He began to regret having taken the dates from him. He would give them back. He had to respond to the insult by returning them. People were impossible to deal with—they give generously to you with one hand, and stab you with another. But Ukhayyad did not give the dates back. He could not bring himself to go back. The memory of his child's cries at home forced him to swallow the insult. The boy had been born sickly like Ukhayyad's mother—skinny and pale, weak in heart and body, beset by sorrow. Since his birth, he had never once smiled. He did nothing but cry. The sound of a home filled with crying children is the only thing that can drive a free man to sell his purebred mount at the public market.

That night, Ayur stepped up her campaign against him, building upon what the peasant had said, "We will not starve to death as long as that Mahri wanders freely in front of our home." This was the last thing he had expected her to say. A well-born woman would never ask for Mahri flesh, even if she were dying of hunger. What kind of woman would crave Mahri flesh?

She was silent for a moment, then followed with another thrust of the knife: "We have eaten nothing but alfalfa for the past few days. Like sheep."

He tried to choke down the pain but could not. He leaped up and sarcastically said, "How do you expect us to go into the desert to use those three bullets if we have nothing to ride?" He could not escape the contempt he felt toward the woman, toward himself, toward children, toward the whole world. From the moment they emerge from their mother's bellies, humans never truly enjoy a single moment in peace. As soon as they put one calamity behind them, they greet the next. At first they must struggle against the drought, then against the Italians. Then they have to go from the pangs of thirst to the torture of hunger. From the scoldings of fathers to the resentment of wives. From the harshness of the desert outside to the ulcers that burned inside the belly. That is how it is—each thing in its own turn. Yes, the troubles of the outside world might subside—but only so that troubles at home might begin.

In the grove, he vomited. Whenever contempt raged in his insides, this happened. He did not vomit food, but yellow bile. With it, the disease inside came spilling out.

Late that night, he came back and slept outside the hut. For two days after that, Ayur exchanged not a single word with him.

It was then that her kinsman, the stranger, returned to the oasis. Dudu went to the market and bartered two camels for some goods. Ukhayyad met him at the entrance to the market, and there he arrived at an inspired, face-saving solution. Foreigners do not understand the language of borrowing and lending, especially if they are wealthy. Ukhayyad would pawn the piebald to the man. In exchange, he would borrow a camel or two until the war subsided. Then, with luck, he would ransom the Mahri. For this loan, he would put up the most handsome Mahri in the entire Sahara as security. When Ukhayyad spoke to Dudu about the deal, he saw the spark in the man's eyes. It was the kind of glitter that only ever flashed in the eyes of merchants who had lifelong experience trafficking in gold. It was the glitter of gold itself. Was it greed? Ukhayyad told himself that the arrangement would sustain his family until their luck changed. And at the same time, it guaranteed that he would be able to hold on to the piebald.

But Ukhayyad made one mistake: he did not understand what traders meant when they talked about offering something up as security.

O people! This she-camel of God is a sign unto you. Let her feed on God's earth. Do her no harm, lest a swift penalty afflict you!

The Qur'an, 11:64

18

Before leaving, Ukhayyad went off to be alone with the Mahri. In the morning, he prepared himself for their private ritual. He went to the grove and begged for a handful of green alfalfa to bribe the camel with at evening. "As you can see, no sooner do we escape from one trap than we fall into another," he told the camel. "Still, be patient. Didn't you and I agree to be patient? Patience is life—we learned that together long ago."

He patted the animal's neck, and the piebald stopped its chewing. "Sometimes in this world, friends are split apart, and distance must take its share," Ukhayyad continued. "But don't be afraid. Our separation won't last long. We'll meet up again when the smoke clears and when those wretched men stop their war against us. The war can't last forever."

Overcome with fear, the camel protested: "A-a-a . . . ."

He swallowed what was in his mouth, and rejected the proposition: "Aw-a-a-a-a-a-a."

Ukhayyad tried to placate him: "This isn't how nobles behave. Children cry and women cry. Grown men remain steadfast and patient." He wiped his hands on his robe, and buried his head in its wide, loose sleeve. Man and animal embraced for a long time in the night silence.

The foreigner took the camel with him when he left the next morning. He fitted out the camel, complete with saddlebag and a harness decorated with strips of colored leather. Still, the man did not mount the camel. Instead, he tied the purebred Mahri to the tail of his own dirty mongrel. They departed for the Danbaba desert where they joined up with his herd.

But even Ukhayyad, who had been raised with camels, did not know the true extent of the animal's character. He did not know what it meant to befriend a purebred Mahri camel. Just three weeks after leaving, the piebald returned. By that time, Ukhayyad had traded one of the two camels for dates and barley to stem the hunger of Ayur's mouth and eyes. Using the one remaining camel, he plowed water channels for the peasants in exchange for a quarter portion of their harvests. He was out the door at dawn only to return, exhausted, in the evening. Then he would collapse and sleep like a dead man. He was content to wear himself out and sleep soundly. He had forgotten the last time he had enjoyed such deep sleep—throughout the time of famine, an obstinate insomnia had lorded over him. It had been his family, not the hunger, that was stealing his sleep. But now, able to fill his wife's mouth and eyes, he could drift off as soon as he lay down. That pleased him, but at the same time it bothered him. He felt an unfathomable sense of dread—perhaps because he sensed his conflicting feelings might be a signal and he feared such warnings. The desert had taught him to be attuned to them, that in life, nothing was more formidable than a sign, especially if you ignored it or failed to recognize it in the first place.

Signs are fate—or so the desert told him.

Like any creature exhausted from long running, Ukhayyad began to relax as soon as his problems had disappeared behind a sand dune. His actions grew careless. Troubles return quickly to those who slacken their guard against them. If they cannot beat you in fighting face to face, they melt away—and when you turn your back on them, they return to attack you from behind.

These are lessons the desert teaches herders every day, free of charge. But this fickle advisor abandons men as soon as they begin to take up residence in oases, and arrogantly take up tilling the land.

This is what happened to Ukhayyad. Life in the oasis had dressed his slackness in something peasants call 'ease.' Ease is what conceals laxity. And in laxity hides rust.

The row woke him up at dawn. In the sweet intoxication of sleep, Ukhayyad thought he heard the bellowing of an enraged camel. He emerged from the hut to see the shadows of two camels struggling in the twilight, one attacking the other with its teeth. He rubbed his eyes in disbelief. The shadowy figure had the same frame and stature as his piebald. It was the piebald. He had overpowered his opponent, and was clinging onto him. His neck and left upper lip were spattered with blood. In the morning light, Ukhayyad discovered other bite wounds across the other camel's body, and a serious gash under its chest.

Two days later, one of the camel herders arrived and said Dudu had sent him after the escaped Mahri. The man's mouth was empty, toothless. Despite that, he never stopped laughing or chewing tobacco. He sat under a low, shady palm in the field.

"Praise God," he said, taking a pouch from his pocket. "He's let me live long enough to see tobacco become cheap as dirt. Would you believe that a peasant at the grove gave me two handfuls for free?"

The man fell over backwards laughing, exposing his empty gums. Then he went on, "The war may have brought famine, but it also killed the price of tobacco—it's one of the war's genuine benefits. On the coasts, they only smoke cigarettes now. Have you ever tried a cigarette?"

"I don't use tobacco."

"Forgive me. I'm an addict. For me, tobacco comes before everything else. In the desert, I know how to live off herbs for months and years. But I can't go one day without tobacco. You know, people like me commit heinous crimes if they can't get it. Did you ever hear the story of that migrant who was an addict? Some peasants refused to give him tobacco, and he killed them all. He killed three men on account of tobacco leaf. Of course, that's insanity—but it's the sort I can understand!"

Then he laughed again.

That evening, the man told Ukhayyad stories about famine in the desert. He said that in recent years entire families had perished and were then buried in mass graves. In the southern deserts, only sparse rains had fallen—and drought had settled in early with the brutal summer. Everybody had fled the smell of gunpowder, abandoning the verdant pastures of the north. The northern reaches of the Hamada desert were completely empty this year.

"Is there any sign the war might end?" Ukhayyad asked him. "Just the opposite. Weeks ago, emissaries from the resistance traveled around the desert looking to conscript men. They want to bolster their ranks in Kufra oasis and Cyrenaica."

He grew silent for a while. "It doesn't seem that the war will end anytime soon," he finally said, with a tone of dismay. The two men became lost in their thoughts, wandering far, far away. The herder chuckled, "But the upside of the war is that it has destroyed the price of tobacco. Famine doesn't bother me, and now that tobacco is plentiful, I won't have to kill anyone like that migrant did."

"Let's not talk about that for now," Ukhayyad interrupted, "Tell me about the piebald. What's his life like there?"

"Ah. He's no camel, you know. He's a human being in a camel's skin. I've spent my entire life around camels, but I'd never seen one like him before. When Dudu first fetched him, he refused to graze. I saw the sadness in his eyes. I knew he was pining for you. The ability to feel longing is what sets the rare breeds apart from others. Did you know—he even refused to kneel! He's been standing on his feet throughout these past weeks. I tethered him in a nearby pasture, but he broke the cords and raced off toward you. We caught up with him after a fierce chase, and brought him back to the pastures. That time around, we tied him with palm rope instead of camel-hair cord. I'm sorry I had to be so rough with him, but there was no other solution. Do you know what he did? When he couldn't break the rope with his legs, he chewed through it. Then he bolted. We never caught him. He is no camel—he's a human being."

In the darkness Ukhayyad said, "I told him that patience is the only talisman that can protect us from disaster. He must have lost it."

"I don't understand."

Ukhayyad mumbled some incomprehensible words. To which the herder replied, in a knowing tone, "I don't understand how you allowed yourself to pawn him. A Mahri like him should have never been put up for anything."

In his mind, Ukhayyad answered, "I did it because of my family. My wife. What do you know about children or wives?"

Ukhayyad envied this unfettered man who had no cares beyond his handful of tobacco. He had once been as free as the herder and even freer—needing nothing at all, not even tobacco. With the piebald, he had wandered God's wide desert. But then woman appeared and separated him from tribe and companion. Didn't Sheikh Musa say that it was woman who drove Adam from the garden of paradise?

19

ess than a month later, the piebald returned again and the
same herder came looking for him.

The third time he came back, Ukhayyad asked the faqih
to write an amulet that would protect the camel from harm.
After hearing the man's story, the faqih said, "This camel will
not forget, and I do not know how to erase memories. You need
someone else."

The black slaves told him to go see one of the African magi-
cians. But the soothsayer from Tiba, the one who had left
shortly before the famine, had been the last witch in the oasis.
And now that on account of the war the desert caravans had
stopped moving, he had little hope in finding the sorcerers that
used to accompany them.

He took two handfuls of barley while Ayur was not looking and decided to go himself to Danbaba. While they were
alone on the road, Ukhayyad began to scold the animal:
"Don't you realize you're wearing me out? Didn't we agree
that our separation would be just temporary? You have forgotten how to be patient—and you've made us the laughing
stock of everybody."

The animal's eyes glistened with tears, but Ukhayyad showed no mercy: "You run after me like a puppy. That's something that dogs do, not camels!"

Then, softening his tone: "The war will end soon and our life will return to how it was before. Nothing lasts forever, so be patient. Until you do, nothing will straighten out. That was the deal we made!"

He took out his surprise gift. He spread out the barley in front of the Mahri, but the animal turned away, grumbling and fixing his gaze on the horizon.

Ukhayyad knew that the animal did not like what he had said. The piebald began to chew without swallowing, churning up a shiny froth around his mouth. He drooled bits of froth on Ukhayyad's face and limbs, and the young man realized that the camel was burning with anger. Whenever rage ate at him, he vomited up frothy mucus.

He fastened the cord around the camel's forelegs. He forced each leg until it bent, and hobbled each with palm rope so the animal would not get away during the night and attack the other camel. This precaution was necessary since every time the piebald returned from exile, he had viciously pounced on the camel that had taken his place.

Ukhayyad left him there and returned to his gear. He lay down on his arm and tried, without success, to sleep. All through the night he listened to the piebald as he nervously chewed, chomping jerkily at nothing but air and spit. That night, when he discovered he was no longer able to stand their being apart, Ukhayyad decided to retrieve the camel, whatever the cost.

He thought it strange that he had not allowed himself to make this decision before now. But he finally realized, as he rested on the bed of the endless desert, that he would never forgive himself if he failed to retrieve the camel on this trip. The calamity that brought them together in the past had joined their lives in a bond that would last forever. Their bond would surely withstand the famine that today tried to break them apart.

While they were on that immortal journey—going from the tribe's encampments to the fields of Maimoun, from the pastures to the well, and finally from the abyss back to the mouth of the well again—they had purchased life at severe cost. With pain equal to death, with death itself, they had bought their lives and were born anew. Today, how could he let family and famine betray this divine gift that had joined their fates? How had the woman so blinded him from seeing his foul deed for what it was? If not for her, he would not have forgotten to fulfill his pledge to Tanit. If not for her, the curse would not have fallen on him—the curse that blinded him from seeing what he was doing. If not for her, his son would never have come into this world to shackle his neck and hands and feet with chains stronger than iron. This son had not just shackled limbs, but had paralyzed his mind and cloaked his heart. Sons may be the security of fathers—but they are also their undoing.

For those who love, life exists only in death. You cannot hold the heart of the beloved without having first lost your own.

Jalal al-Din al-Rumi, from the *Couplets*

20

You hear the strangest things from the mouths of strangers. "I knew this was going to happen," Dudu told him at the outset. "I saw it in your eyes. I saw it in his eyes."

"The hardship we shared transformed us from two creatures into one. I hope you can understand when I say that he and I should not be apart from one another."

"Why didn't you say so when the hunger began to gnaw at you?"

"It's in a father's nature to lose his mind when he hears his son cry. And now the matter rests in your hands. Don't forget that he's the one who pulled me out of the well. He's the one who gave me my life. Put yourself in my place."

The man was silent for a while. Then he said, "I'll send you my response tomorrow."

The next day, Ukhayyad heard the most incredible thing, though not directly from the mouth of the man himself. Instead, it was delivered by a messenger—the same laughing, toothless herder as before. The old man sat, stirring his evening tea. "He'll give the piebald back to you on the condition that you divorce his kinswoman," he said, with the studied foolishness of herders. He said it just like that, without preface or sense of shame.

Ukhayyad didn't understand at first. So the herder repeated his master's pronouncement a second, then a third time.

After a long silence, Ukhayyad asked, "What's the one thing got to do with the other?"

"Since he made it a condition, there must be some connection. Only God knows the intentions of foreigners."

"Imposing conditions on other people may be permitted by holy law, but only barely so. Is this how Muslims should treat one another?"

"Depending on the circumstance, Islam and holy law can be disregarded."

"If I had my rifle with me, he would not have dared to send this message."

"Even if you were holding your rifle in your hands this very minute, you couldn't do a thing. His money has brought him servants and slaves and herdsmen—an entire retinue gathered with gold. He's more powerful than you—and he's got the piebald."

The herder offered Ukhayyad a cup of tea. "You should not have pawned this jewel to him," he repeated with the same brusque tone as before. "If you had pawned him to me, I'd have done the same, I'd think up devilish tricks to steal him away from you." He smiled mysteriously and blew on his tea. "Always treat a foreigner as an opponent. Men never go into exile without good reason. And in the heart of every foreigner sleeps a secret."

Ukhayyad did not blow on his tea, but let the cup sit buried in the sand. He listened to the bubbles of the foam as they scattered and popped. In the excruciating silence, even this sound could be clearly heard.

The herder said, "The truth is he told me something else I never thought to tell you before."

"You can speak frankly with me. Nothing will shock me like this proposition he's made."

"Then don't be surprised by what I say—strange things come from strangers." Before going on, the man blew on his tea cup with an annoying sound. "He wants to marry her according to the customs of God and His Prophet."

Ukhayyad shot him a look of utter disbelief. The herder looked down and closed his eyes. "Marry his kin," he said, pretending to busy himself with the teacups. "He said he'd marry her according to the custom of God and His Prophet. There's no shame in that, is there?"

"But I love her," Ukhayyad shouted. "Did someone tell him I didn't love her?"

"And he also loves her. That's what he said. And blood relatives, by custom, have precedence—he also said that."

"If only I had my rifle . . ."

"You wouldn't do a thing. He's got his men and bodyguards, his servants, and slaves. With his money and his gold, he's bought everything."

"God damn him and his gold. Does he think he can buy me— me!—and buy my wife with his gold?"

"He did buy you. He bought you the day you placed your piebald in his hands. As for your wife, he'll get her from you too. He's related to her, he's kin. He'll get her back from you and go back to Aïr with her. And he'll do all this according to the law of God and His Prophet. What in this could anger God or mankind?"

"Did he say he was going to take her back to Aïr?"

"Yes."

"What about my son? The boy is my son."

"He'll live in Dudu's care as if he were his own son. He'll live in comfort ever after. And, when he grows up, you can go retrieve him if you wish. That's what Dudu said. He's left nothing out of his proposition, as you can see. Didn't I tell you that foreigners hide great secrets?"

"I'll fight him. I'll take back the piebald by force. When there's no more sense of shame, force becomes the law of the desert. You know what I mean."

"Force won't accomplish anything. With his money and his men, he is much more powerful than you are."

"Don't forget I've got my tribe. The most powerful tribe . . . "

"Your tribe was scattered by the Italians—and he knows that. He also knows that your father, mercy on his soul, wasn't pleased when you married his kin. I overheard Dudu repeating your father's curse more than once, 'Marry her and be damned.' I don't know where he heard it. But, as you know, nothing remains hidden forever, not even in the desert. Didn't I tell you there was a great secret sleeping in the man's heart?"

But Ukhayyad was to hear another strange thing a few moments later.

"I forgot to ask him what exactly their relationship is," Ukhayyad said as darkness began to shroud the expanse of the horizon. "I never asked her either."

The herder blurted out, "She's his paternal cousin."

"His cousin?"

"Yes. Dudu has been in love with her since they were children. The two fathers had a falling out and the two were separated from one another. It's not surprising that her father would refuse to let her marry him. When her father died, her clan left for Azjar. During that time, Dudu was being held prisoner among the Bambara tribes. He had gone on a raid to steal gold and fell into an ambush. Years later, he managed to escape. He returned to Aïr and discovered that she had gone. He gathered his vassals and attacked the Bambara—and took that cursed gold as his prize. He then sold it in Ghadamès, and you know the rest of the story. He said that the reason he had gone after the gold was to secure a dowry. This is only part of the man's secret. As for the rest, it remains concealed and only God knows what it is."

Ukhayyad was utterly astonished. He doubled over low, like a dervish in the throes of ecstasy. "You were right," he said. "A man doesn't leave his country without good reason. You were right—secrets sleep in the heart of the foreigner."

21

The piebald caught up with Ukhayyad less than a week after he returned to the oasis. This time the camel arrived in a much worse state. Ukhayyad had never seen him in this condition before. He had become so emaciated his ribs stuck out. His eyes were sunken in hollow sockets. His forelegs were covered with deep gashes, the wounds of palm rope, the coarsest kind of rope there is. They had rebranded the camel on his left shank as well, changing the '+' brand of his tribe to '11+,' the mark used by the tribes of Aïr.

This was a sign from Dudu, the clever fox. It was a provocation. Dudu wanted to say that the Mahri did not belong to Ukhayyad anymore. Allowing the camel to come after him was itself a sign from one who wanted to put a flame to Uhkayyad's heart.

When your beloved is far away, separation is bearable. Out of sight, out of mind. But to see the beloved is for passion to rekindle. This was the trick Dudu was playing. The herder had been right, the heart of the stranger is the refuge of unknowable schemes. When they parted, the herder told him, "You should not have pawned a Mahri like this to a foreigner. The likes of him should be kept hidden from the eyes of strangers. But what's done is done." The man spat out some of his chewing tobacco as he left to rejoin his herd.

Ukhayyad thought he would never see this herder again. He assumed that, after his master's crazy proposition, the herder's sense of dignity would suffice to make him leave Danbaba for good. It was a shameful demand. The first time Dudu had come to the oasis and stayed as a guest, Ukhayyad had not noticed anything wrong in either his appearance or behavior. All that he had noticed was that, in addition to the veil made of ashen cloth, the man wore a second, more impenetrable veil. Ukhayyad did not claim to know much about the hearts of men, but Dudu's gloomy silence and unease had betrayed this second veil, the one that cloaked his heart.

The eyes are the mirror of the heart, as everyone knows, and while you can disguise your face behind a veil, you cannot hide the heart—for it speaks through the eyes. When Dudu had greeted Ayur, he was formal, even ceremonial—and nothing in his behavior aroused any suspicion except his fingertips. Etching his index finger into the ground, Dudu traced the sacred triangle for a while, then nervously went back over it, erasing the figure of Tanit he had just drawn. In that instant, a tremble shot through his fingers. At the time, Ukhayyad had not recognized the sign. But now, after thinking about it so intently, and after this latest secret had been divulged, he could see Dudu's behavior for what it was. How fantastic the secrets of strangers are! And how strong these men are because of it! He who knows how to conceal his secrets is always the strongest.

That day Ukhayyad attempted to test his strength. He decided to abandon the Mahri for good. If he did not do it now, the shame of Dudu's insult would stick to him forever. The desert was a merciless place. When the curse of shame sticks to a person there, he is stricken from memory. Worse, the scorn becomes inscribed, not only upon him, but upon his progeny as well. In the code of the desert, it is more merciful to be blotted out from the minds of men than it is to suffer this kind of scorn. A man scorned suffers not the finality of a single death, but rather death hundreds and thousands of times over—every day, every hour, every moment of his life. A real man, a man with dignity, chooses to die once rather than a thousand times. The thousandfold death is fit for slaves, and maybe vassals—but not self-respecting nobles.

In the morning, Ukhayyad placed the saddle and baggage on the plow camel and stole off, before the eye could distinguish the white thread from the black one in the twilight gloom. He descended into an arid valley and thrust his foot into the neck of the camel, spurring him into a trot. At that moment, he heard a distant howl of pain, "Aw-a-a-a-a-a."

The wail came from far away, but the complaint and torment it communicated shot across the open desert to Ukhayyad. Only pain can turn the bellowing of camels into the howls of wolves. The piebald always howled when he complained, but he never complained unless the pain touched his heart. There is no creature in this world who can bear corporeal pain like a camel. At the same time, there is no creature as weak as a camel when it comes to heartache. Ukhayyad knew this from his experience with the piebald.

As he listened to the wail and his heart split in two, he tried to snuff out the pain that sparked in his core. It quickly ignited a fire whose flames consumed his breast. He whipped the plow camel's shanks, spurring him to gallop on. He wanted to flee far, far away. He wanted to disappear, he wanted the sound of the camel to fade away and the fire inside him to die out. But the more pain flooded in, the more memories began to pour out. As if in a dream, he saw their friendship as it had been at the very beginning, before they were born, before they were clots in their mothers' wombs. He saw them together, before they were even a thought, or a feeling, in their fathers' hearts. He saw them before they were a desire that took hold of bodies, before they were even dust drifting in the endless void. He could glimpse them back when they had been merely a sound in the wind, the echo of a song, the lamentation of strings played between the fingers of a beautiful woman, and the trilling of a houri in paradise. Yes, that was it—the sublime sound of a merciful houri singing in the shadows of the well. And now he saw it clearly: before they ever existed as anything, they had been as one being.

How could he go off now—cloaked in the darkness of dawn, fleeing like a thief—abandoning the Mahri? How could Ukhayyad throw him off, as he might toss away a ring from his finger? How could he cast him to the barbarians in the Danbaba desert? Could a woman, a boy, and a stupid thing that people in the brutal desert called 'shame' make him abandon his divine half and trade it for the illusion of the world? And what was a woman? She was the noose Satan created so that he could lead men around by their necks! What was a son? The toy fathers play with, thinking they will find immortality and salvation—while in actuality they find instead the ruination of their wealth and life!

And what was shame? Another illusion created by the people of the desert so as to shackle themselves with chains and rope.

If this is what shame really was, then dignity was freedom. Dignity meant saving the companion he had known in death. The companion who had carried him across the desert realms throughout these years. Dignity meant giving up the noose, the toy, and the illusion. It meant choosing the piebald. It meant that the two of them had to resume their journey across the desert realms.

Abruptly, he choked back the reins and turned on his heels. Dudu received him with the rising sun, wearing a linen veil over his face and a second over his heart. But, Ukhayyad now saw the ridicule in the man's eyes, the confident disdain of one who knew that he had won. For a second, Dudu's eyes gleamed a knowing smile, and then that smile vanished. Only at that moment did Ukhayyad begin to hate the man. This feeling of hate jolted through him as quick as lightning, as quick as Dudu's concealed smile. Ukhayyad was astonished that until now he had never felt any hatred toward him. He had grown angry when the herder told him Dudu's proposal, but he had not felt hate or resentment at the time. Perhaps because the guileless herdsman had succeeded so well in convincing him that the crisis had come about from his own mistake, the mistake of pawning the piebald. The herder had talked with him for a long while about the magical significance that the word 'pawn' had among merchants. The herder told him that Dudu himself had fallen into many traps set for him by the merchants of Timbuktu, Aghadès, and Ghadamès before catching on and learning what this word meant.

Now Ukhayyad also understood the meaning of this curse. Before, he had borne the brunt of the blame for what had happened, but now he understood, and his resentment found its mark: Dudu was to blame for what had happened. The famine was to blame for what had happened. Ayur, the child, the Italians, the desert—they were all to blame. My God—when fate sets things up, it spreads blame all around. It can turn everything against you—people, things, the desert—and arrange it so that no one is to blame for any one thing at all. When everyone shares complicity, there are no culprits. How clever fate can be when it wants to hide its tracks!

Dudu had come pursuing a cousin he had loved since his youth, a cousin who had been separated from him by the machinations of fate. Did Ukhayyad have the right to condemn him? If he were in the man's place, would he treat him as his enemy?

Dudu said, "You came back to check on the giraffe?"

Confused, Ukhayyad asked, "Giraffe?"

"Yes—that is what I call him. The giraffe is the most beautiful animal we have in Aïr."

Ukhayyad asked if he could see the animal. Dudu shook his head. "That won't do anyone any good. Soon, you'll want to come back to him again and again."

Ukhayyad didn't get angry, and said nothing. "He's in the pasture in the western valley," the strange foreigner finally muttered.

Now Ukhayyad understood. The morning breeze had come up from the east. It had been easy for the piebald to catch Ukhayyad's scent when he tried to flee at dawn.

22

As the dreams of night scatter with the glowing embers of dawn, Ukhayyad's resolve vanished as soon as he saw Dudu wrapped in his blue cloak, standing in the doorway. At that moment, he realized that a person is who he is because of what he drinks in his mother's milk. He knew it would be difficult to remove the noose, the toy, and the illusion from his head, unless he were to suddenly become another person altogether. "As a person is prisoner to his body, so too he is hostage to his worldly possessions," Sheikh Musa often liked to say. By that, did he mean that people are unable to change themselves—just as they are unable to trade their bodies for others? But, could he really be content to sell the piebald and surrender himself to them—that noose of a woman, doll of a boy, and illusion of shame? Could he pawn himself to them simply because everybody else does that—abandoning the only sincere friend he had in this world?

Could he commit this betrayal without despising himself?

Descending through the valley, he had no sooner awoken from these thoughts when the Mahri rushed toward him, his forelegs still hobbled, froth spitting, and sweat pouring from his body. There was the old sadness in his eyes. He brought the plow camel to a halt off at a distance, and went down the hill on foot. They embraced.

Ukhayyad meant to be severe with the camel. "Are you a stud or a mare? What you are doing does not befit Mahris. Do you understand? I've told you a hundred times: be patient, it is the only thing that can protect you if you want to survive in the desert. Patience is prayer, it's worship. Have you forgotten our journey to the fields of Maimoun? Have you forgotten our trip to Awal? Forgetting is your weakness and in the desert, it causes nothing but problems."

The camel's heart was not soothed. Distress flickered from his fear-stricken eye sockets. Those eyes spoke as eloquently as those of a gazelle.

Ukhayyad continued to talk to the camel, rubbing him gently, consoling him until midday. But no sooner did Ukhayyad leave than the camel bellowed in complaint. It sounded like the moans of a dying man.

To Ukhayyad's ears, the piebald's cries were unlike those of any other camel.

23

And now here he was, surprising Ukhayyad again.

The camel arrived, weak with fresh wounds, conveying a new message from Dudu. It was a cruel proposal, composed simply of wounds and new misery. This wretched skeleton was a warning, a sign, and it filled Ukhayyad with dread. The desert had taught him to fear this secret language, for it conveyed hidden truth, and it never signified in jest. The language of hidden, divine truth can kill.

Did the foreigner want to murder the piebald, or was this just a new stage of his heartless blackmail? Did he mean to extract revenge on the innocent animal for Ukhayyad's scornful refusal to divorce Ayur, or was torture his method for forcing Ukhayyad into submission?

However much you think about the souls of foreigners, however smart you are, however many times you revise your interpretations, there are always more secrets to be found in them. It does not matter how clever or brilliant you are—the weapons of foreigners are always more lethal than your own. People never go into exile without a reason. The shrewd herder had been right about that.

That day, when the piebald appeared in tatters—emaciated, his bones sticking out—Ukhayyad saw contempt in Ayur's eyes for the first time ever. No—he was not mistaken, she showed it on purpose. The look of contempt is unambiguous. She did not even attempt to hide it. What did it mean? Had something aroused her jealousy? Her jealousy toward the piebald had not been born just today! He was the splendid mount that had made Ukhayyad's warrior status complete long before he got married. But he was also the mount that, after Ukhayyad's marriage, had become like a second wife to her, that is, her opponent and even enemy. She had never dared to talk openly about any of her feelings toward the animal. But with all the hints she gave, it had not been difficult for him to understand where things stood.

They talked one night after dinner, a few months after their wedding, while they were still camping in the Hamada. "In all the desert I have never seen women as jealous as those of your tribe," she told him. "Do you know what Tazidirt told me? She said, 'Watch out. You cannot depend on a man who loves his Mahri the way Ukhayyad loves his piebald. It really is the most splendid Mahri in the desert, but when a rider loves his mount that much, no wife should trust him. Either his heart is with his mount, or it is split between his mount and his wife—and that is even worse! When a man loves his Mahri more than his wife, she should know this: she will soon lose him altogether.' Did you ever hear such a ridiculous thing?"

He laughed that day and told her that Tazidirt was a wise woman who spoke only the truth. She had laughed too—but she never forgave him for turning the matter into a joke.

As soon as the famine began, she found her chance to get rid of the Mahri. At first, she had only insinuated this a number of times. Later, when she could no longer restrain her intentions, she announced her desires plainly and publicly. At the time Ukhayyad forgave her, since he could see what starvation was doing to everybody. He told himself that a mother who had to watch her son crying from hunger certainly had the right to lose her mind.

But now her jealousy was not simply due to his devotion to the piebald. It was because she had seen him struggle so much since pawning the camel to her kinsman. She had seen him advance and retreat as he went back and forth, again and again, between Danbaba and the oasis. She had closely watched his trips there and his returns. She thought it was a disgrace—and that he should be ashamed of himself. This was not just the jealousy a wife might feel toward the mount of a warrior. His stubborn attachment to the animal posed a real danger to her—a danger to her and to the child. She understood this with a woman's intuition—and nothing is more sensitive than a woman who doubts! Her glance today was a warning and challenge—and it communicated contempt. Yes—contempt now flashed within her scorn. What does it mean to feel contempt as well as scorn? Contempt is stronger and crueler than scorn, and is something one suckles from a mother's breast, or from the breast of the desert itself.

My God! Perhaps she truly loved her cousin—and perhaps she had meant to insult Ukhayyad so as to win her divorce papers. This fantastical idea only multiplied Ukhayyad's distress. It dawned on him that all this time she had hidden the nature of her relationship to Dudu. Why had she not told him the whole story? Why, unless she was concealing some secret? Here was woman, the horrible noose tightening around his neck, strangling his breath. Here also the shadows crept up to swallow the light of day. That night, Ukhayyad wept.

Instead of sleep, he found two burning ribbons of tears pouring down his cheeks. He never thought he was capable of crying like this. A descendent of the great Akhenukhen crying in bed like the weakest woman! During his childhood, Ukhayyad had once fought one of his cohort to see who could hold a glowing coal in the palm of his hand the longest. The stench of burning flesh billowed from his hand, but he never let go. His opponent soon collapsed in pain and threw down his coal with a yelp. But Ukhayyad did not scream or cry, even though he was only nine at the time. Another time, when he was seven, his mother punished him by having their African servant insert hot pepper oil into his nostrils—spoonfuls of the stuff. He first passed out, then stopped breathing. But on that day, he did not cry.

Much later, he had plowed a furrow across the desert hanging from the tail of the piebald, then leaped into a bottomless black pit. He had died and returned to live again—all without tears.

Yet, here he was tonight, unable to stop himself. It was as if the person crying was not him, but someone else—his double— sleeping next to him, defying him. Someone else whose activities and deeds he could watch without being seen. Had this ever happened before to anybody in the desert?

He stole out of bed and left the hut. Outside, the glow of dawn began to split the shadows of the oasis, but the cocks had forgotten to announce the day's birth, or maybe they had meant to conceal their secret. Only a band of crickets remained, carrying on with their late-night songs.

The piebald had also spent the night awake. Ukhayyad found him standing erect with his long frame, his head facing east. He was miserable and anxious as he silently watched the dawn's birth. Meanwhile, the plow camel kneeled on the other side of the hut. It sat beside a thick, stooped palm, stupidly, mechanically chewing its cud. At this early hour, the melancholic piebald seemed saint-like in his pose. The other camel, whose mind remained carefree and vacant, seemed brutish and stupid in comparison. How appalling living creatures seem when their hearts are so free of worry or concern! Only sadness can implant the glow of divinity in a heart! Did this apply to people as well? Sheikh Musa always said that God loves only those worshippers who have experienced pain and suffering. Indeed, He inflicts misery only upon those whom He loves! The Sufi sheikhs in the oasis also often talked about something like this.

In the corner of the hut, he stole three handfuls of barley and snatched up his rifle. He attached the bridle through the Mahri's nose and led him along the road to the vineyard spring.

On the road, Ukhayyad found himself repeating a refrain as if he were singing, "Patience is prayer. Patience is worship. Patience is life itself." He took comfort repeating the words into the piebald's ears, telling himself that the song was meant for the suffering Mahri. Inside he knew that this time the words were addressed to himself. That other person who had wept tonight, that other he had discovered living in his body—he was the one chanting the incantation. This other would be the one who would transform his sense of unrest into living deed. Since last night, this other had become his hand, his tongue, his eye. Those eyes with which he had cried—they belonged to this other. How long had this other lived inside his breast—since birth? Why had he woken up only yesterday?

Ukhayyad crossed through the palm forests and drew up beside the southern sand dune. He forced the camel to kneel, then unrolled a tatter of burlap cloth. He pulled out the packet of barley and spread it before the camel. But the piebald turned his nose up with disdain and stared at the desolate horizon.

The first fiery thread of the sun's rays now burst forth. He sat on his toes across from the camel. Leaning on his rifle, Ukhayyad stared intensely at the piebald.

And then, though he did not know how, he raised the barrel of the rifle and pointed it directly at his companion. He stood up slowly, as if being plucked up by strings, and drew the gun barrel toward the camel's head. He took a step forward, then another, until the rifle mouth pressed against the camel's forehead. He clutched the weapon with both hands, and placed it directly between the camel's eyes. Ukhayyad's hands were steady and his eyes shone with resolute determination and something dark. The piebald also surrendered to the moment. Their eyes met. There was no astonishment in the camel's eyes. On the contrary, the camel seemed to bless what was happening. "Pull the trigger," his eyes seemed to encourage Ukhayyad. Those deep eyes were as pure as the water in the vineyard spring, and now they were telling him: "Put out this fire, if you wish to live apart. The shadows that hang about us cannot be worse than the fire of Asyar. They cannot match the cruelty of the road to Awal. Put out this fire inside me!"

Their eyes locked for what seemed like forever. Finally, Ukhayyad's resolve broke, and his hand began to tremble. He shoved the rifle barrel into the sand beside the camel's folded leg and trembled there for a few moments. Then he felt the water begin to roil down his cheeks again. His breast seethed and flared with anger and rage. How would he put out the fire?

He began to bash the rifle butt against his head until his turban fell off. Blow after blow, and the blood began to pour, splattering on his hands, across the sand, and across the burlap cloth and into the barley. Blood splattered over the piebald's face as he nervously watched the burst of madness. With each blow, the distress in his eyes developed into fear. Perhaps this was because he did not know what madness was. Perhaps it was because he believed that man alone was blessed with the gift of reason and that he had no right to lose it and behave like a beast. Ukhayyad had indeed now lost his mind. Who was this person then? What would he do to himself? How far would he go?

The camel suddenly opened his mouth and bellowed, "Aw-a-a-a-a-a-a."

The open desert quickly swallowed the pained cry and Ukhayyad stopped and fell on the sand.

It was now late afternoon.

He found himself in a fever, drenched in sweat and blood. He did not know when or how he had passed out. The pain of the gashes split his head. The time had come for the pains of the body to vanquish those of the heart. If only there was a way for the pains of the body to absorb these others—then no one would ever feel any pain. As soon as he came to and remembered what had happened, his headache dissolved—and with it, the sufferings of his body. Heartache had consumed all other pain.

Ukhayyad went and washed in the vineyard spring. He concealed his wounds beneath his veil and rested in the shady thicket of palms that surrounded the pool of water. He drank, and drenched his chest, clothes, and head with water. He eventually got up and headed for the oasis village.

He found the man he sought sitting in the circle of sheikhs. The cadi was taking refuge from the scorching afternoon sun behind the courtyard wall and was absorbed in fighting off flies with a palm frond swatter. Ukhayyad asked to speak to the man alone, and then demanded a writ of divorce. The cadi attempted to dissuade him, and tried to postpone drafting the document. The man said, "Though frowned upon, a divorce was permitted by God's law. There is nothing easier." It was better—though harder, he said—to restrain one's impulses than regret one's actions later. But, confronted with Ukhayyad's determination, the cadi abandoned his sermon and resorted to a trick that he thought would delay the process and muddle Ukhayyad's passion: he demanded that a witness be present. Ukhayyad went out and grabbed the first peasant he met in the square, dragging him back to the cadi. "When Satan sets his heart on something, he makes it happen," the cadi sighed. "When he wants to push someone over a cliff, he removes all the obstacles that stand in his way. May God prevail!" He then gave the ill-omened document to Ukhayyad, who then folded it, pressed it into his pocket, and departed for Danbaba.

He met alone with Dudu and handed him the paper, the document of his surrender and deliverance. The writ was his emancipation from the noose, the doll, and the illusion—forever. Dudu was ecstatic. He ordered his servants to bring some tea and prepare them supper. "I knew you'd do it," he exclaimed. "And it's a good thing you did, too. You have broken your fetters and regained a true friend. I could see it in your eyes and his since the very first day. The truth was right there, hidden in your eyes."

He smiled and went on, "Who would ever trade a giraffe like this piebald of yours for a woman, even if she were a goddess of beauty like Tanit? God forbid you ever did such a thing! But isn't our entire fate inscribed on our foreheads for all to see?"

From an iron box he took out an old leather pouch engraved with magic amulets. He dipped a teacup into it twice. The gold dust flashed, blinding the eye.

The yellow rays of twilight were reflected in the yellow specks and, in seeming response, the gold appeared to radiate from within.

Dudu pushed the pouch toward Ukhayyad, saying, "Don't think of this as a bribe. Think of it as protection from the evil of necessity until the famine has passed."

Ukhayyad answered, "I don't think I'll need it. In our tribe, gold is said to bring bad luck."

The man ignored the second half of what Ukhayyad had just said. Instead, he commented on the first part: "Not only do humans need gold, but jinn need it as well. It is the source of the struggles between humans and jinn, between humans and Satan, and also among humans. How could you not need it? Because of it, I was held prisoner and tortured by the blacks of Bambara. But also, without it, I could not have accomplished what I have."

He waved the piece of paper in the air and smiled. Ukhayyad reminded him with naive determination, "But they say it is cursed and brings bad luck."

"Those are myths spread by people incapable of attaining it. Gold is the goal of every person, from when they are born till the moment they die. It's what everyone wants, everyone that is, except losers and Sufi dervishes. Losers and dervishes revile it and spread their nasty rumors about it for only one reason: they don't know how to get it! Believe me!"

A flash sparkled in the man's eye as he spoke.

24

I n the fertile southern pastures below Jebel Hasawna, the
piebald recovered his vigor.

One low-lying valley in particular had received the rains of
passing clouds at the end of last spring. None of the experienced herders had gone there, because the rains had arrived so
late. After leaving Adrar for the northern desert, Ukhayyad had
stumbled upon this valley. He had decided to stay put there.
Leaving the camel in the green pasture he took refuge in a cave
on the western slopes.

He decided to settle here, not only because the place was a
reward from God, a green treasure hidden from other travelers
and herdsmen, but also because he had discovered another
treasure there as well—desert truffles. He had not eaten them
since settling in the wretched oasis. Once a man has tried such
truffles, he spends the rest of his life longing to taste them
again.

In those hidden fields, the piebald recovered his muscle, fat,
and gleaming coat—and Ukhayyad savored truffles for the first
time since his long exile in the oases. The truffles were like a
reward for all his patience and suffering.

But the real compensation was not to be found in the truffles, nor in the piebald's regained health. The prize was in the pure presence of God that can be found only in the quiet emptiness of infinite wilderness. Only those who have been shackled by life in the oasis can know the meaning of serenity. Such serenity means nothing to those who have not experienced the fetters of family and shame, not to mention the worries of life and the machinations of men. By day, such men labor stubbornly. By night, they are insomniacs—and their chains become only tighter and more jagged. As soon as such a man breaks one knot, he discovers new fetters around his hands and feet, strangling him like serpents. They are like drowning men—however much they raise their heads and dream of rescue, strong currents tug them under. People say that in the vineyard spring there lives a demon who is skilled at this kind of sport. He does not try to drown his victims unless they come to swim alone. He never attacks those who come to swim in groups.

These are the traps of sedentary life in the oasis generally— for that demon did not just haunt the vineyard spring, but the entire oasis.

Here, on the other hand, demons die of thirst, leaving two expanses to reveal themselves—that of the open desert and that of the heart. Here, there was a stillness of the ears, and a stillness of the heart. There was God's presence in the desert, and His presence inside a man's chest. And while the waters of the vineyard spring may wash clean the body, only the desert can cleanse the soul. In the desert, the soul empties and clears and becomes free and brave in the process. And so it enables you to defy the endless open space, challenge the horizon, and explore the emptiness that leads beyond the horizon, beyond the desert void. It invites you to face the other world, the hereafter. It was here, only here, in the labyrinths of never-ending desert plains, that the extremes converge—open expanse, horizon, and desolation—to form a firmament that expands outward, toward eternity, toward the afterlife.

This celestial union weaves together the threads of God's presence, and plants stillness and calm in the heart. He had heard Sheikh Musa repeat this mantra so often that Ukhayyad began to think it was a sura from the Qur'an—the Sura of Serenity. He had never known what it meant until now—after tasting life in the oases, after wrapping himself in devilish chains like everybody else does in the world. He had traded his freedom for a noose and a doll and an illusion, and told himself the same story as everybody else, "This is what we found our forefathers doing." Now, he grasped the meaning of this mantra. When he heard it from Sheikh Musa and learned it by heart, he never realized that he would someday be traveling down the road it described: *Abraham's people stubbornly insisted on worshiping idols simply because they inherited the custom from father to son.* Meanwhile, Ukhayyad had done the same: he married and begot a child and built a special place in his heart for shame—so as to confine himself with fetters stronger than any iron chain.

He forgot about the verse, the sura, the magic spell. He forgot about the words that opened up secrets—serenity, freedom, the presence of God. He had forgotten them simply because he had left the desert and placed his neck in the shackles of settled life in the oases. The inhabitants of the oases were nothing but slaves. No one but a slave would agree to live behind walls or under a mud roof. And Ukhayyad had been a unique kind of slave—a blind one. He had been unable to recognize that his own soul was being enslaved. He had not been slave to another man, but slave to a devil, which was surely worse. A man who is slave to other men arouses pity, but a slave to demons makes you cringe with disgust. The piebald had saved Ukhayyad from this repugnant form of slavery—he was a divine messenger. Were it not for the pure animal, he would have continued following in Satan's tracks, and perished along with so many other lost souls. The piebald was his savior, the vessel that would deliver him to freedom. And here they were, racing like gazelles across God's wide desert—that everlasting desert stretching from here to the hereafter.

Goodbye broken chains. Goodbye to the cage whose bars were stronger than those of the prisons the last Ottoman governor left behind when they evacuated the oasis.

The honor of breaking from that cage went to the piebald. And now God had rewarded the camel for his patience and led him to this treasure—to these hidden pastures. The pastures that the passing clouds had made so verdant. The green was heaven's gift in the desert. Even the barren desert knew how to hide surprises to reward those who are patient. It had rewarded the Mahri with sweet grasses, and Ukhayyad with truffles.

If truffles were not precious treasure, then what was? A fruit that fell from heaven? It is nothingness that brings truffles forth in great abundance. The earth splits apart to let them come up. Their strong earthy scent wafts across the land. The winds scatter them and carry them back to earth. Then lightning mixes with thunder and suddenly the magical fruit is born again in the heart of the void. To enjoy truffles at the outset of summer— that was a mercy from heaven. This was paradise on earth.

But had paradise lasted even until the days of the ancients? And had God's blessings survived even into the age of the Prophets?

25

One day, one of the deep desert herdsmen stumbled into Ukhayyad's paradise. The man rode in at nightfall on a stout, disheveled camel. He tethered the beast in the field and called out, "Praise God!" three times before greeting Ukhayyad. He said he was looking for his lost camels. He also said that Ukhayyad must be a saint beloved of God, since he had been blessed above all others with such pasturage—especially with the other parts of the desert world suffering from such drought.

Ukhayyad invited him to share tea. "It's best if you say nothing about this to anyone," Ukhayyad said.

"I'll keep it a secret if you let me graze my camels here," the stranger laughed, and then added, "That is, if God helps me find them in His wide desert!"

"God willing, you will find them."

"No doubt I will. God answers the prayers of His saints."

He wiped his beard and leaned back contentedly on the pebbles beneath them. "I'll keep it a secret if you let me graze," he repeated. "As you can see, I don't ask for much in exchange for my silence!"

Laughing again, he said, "To be content with what we have. The faqihs all agree in their condemnation of greed—and who am I to say otherwise? To hell with wealth! Did you hear the story about that man in Adrar oasis who sold his wife and child for a handful of gold dust?"

The blood froze in Ukhayyad's veins. "What!" he gasped.

"The story is on everyone's tongue. The man surrendered his wife and child to one of the rich foreigners for a handful of gold dust. Gold—it blinds the eye! Not until I heard that story did I realize how cursed that yellow copper truly is."

Ukhayyad held his tongue. Cold sweat poured across his shoulders, soaking the skin. His hands trembled and tea spilled onto the ground. Soon, the perspiration began to seep from his forehead and from around his mouth. Beads of it dripped into the cups, mixing into the frothy crown of the green tea. Blood began to seep from his heart.

In that single instant, he forgot all about the burdens sons inherit from their fathers—the nooses that choke, the dolls that bring ruin, and the empty, empty illusions. The things of the world began to take on their old meanings again. The noose went back to being a beloved wife. The doll became, once more, his progeny and heir to his mantle. The sham illusion became, once again, shame—actual shame.

In the blink of an eye, the beautiful dream melted away. In the blink of an eye, a harsh, wretched truth settled in. As the vision disappeared, freedom dissolved and the shackles returned.

It seemed to him now that all he had thought about during his daring escape had been no more than a fantasy. His wife was no noose, but a refuge; his son, no plaything, but the awaited messiah. The illusion too was revealed for what it was. In an instant, every sign turned on its head.

There was nothing strange about this turn of events. When a person decides to oppose Satan, he should never let his guard down. In order to converse with another living creature, a person has to speak in the Devil's tongue. And in that moment, all vision of the divine vanishes, and all signs of heaven disappear.

How did this wretched nomad know how to banish inspiration? How did that accursed man know so well how to drive him mad?

26

For three consecutive nights he dreamed of the same decrepit house.

He did not actually sleep. The burning that filled his heart left no room for slumber. But with the glow of each new dawn, he managed to drift off for a short spell. And there, in his sleep, he saw the wretched ruins. Though he knew this fitful sleep would be fleeting, his wanderings through the wrecked dwelling would last the whole night.

The dream was not new.

In his childhood, it had tortured him again and again, returning to torment him during the first years of his youth. At that time, he had not yet visited the oases, nor ever once seen a house built with adobe or stone. Even so, the vision haunted him. The dark, foreboding house had two stories, and was built of mud brick. Its roof was made of palm trunks, over which rested a layer of palm fronds, and clay mixed with earth. The ground floor was a shambles. A wall, and some of the rooms too, had partly collapsed. There was something else about the house: it was completely abandoned and had neither windows nor doors. It was strange: Ukhayyad always found himself trapped inside without knowing how he had got in. He was on the second floor walking along dark hallways looking for a way out—a door or window or even a glint of light. The ground beneath him shook and threatened to collapse, and he would step faster, holding his breath for fear of falling. At the same time, he instinctively felt the presence of a specter that never actually appeared, neither as substance nor shadow. In the dream, these two fears were always with him, that he would fall and that he would enrage the phantom being.

Later in his youth, the dream abruptly stopped. After that he forgot all about it.

This was the dream that came back the first night after talking with the traveler. That night, something snatched his sleep away. And now, only now, could he clearly make out the three things that had so frightened him: the obscurity, the rickety ceiling, and the shadowy being that had never—not in the past, nor in the latest visitations—announced itself by word or by sign. Ukhayyad knew that it was present somewhere in the house, at the end of one of the hallways, in the corner of one of the rooms, in the ceiling, on the rooftop, or on the ground floor below amid the debris and piles of fallen bricks. He dreaded this being—its mere presence filled his heart with a terror, a dread that made him feel ashamed upon awaking. He had never experienced this kind of fear in his waking life. Even death never aroused feelings like this in him. What was he afraid of? Who, or what was this being? Was it human or jinn? Angel or devil?

As he struggled, searching for the being, the same two things stood in his way: the gloom and the ceiling that was always on the verge of collapse. His steps were anxious and hesitant. The sweat poured out of him, he panted, and groped along the empty hallways like a blind man. For some reason, he would not use his hands to feel his way along the walls. Instead, he walked feebly and alone into the void, always about to tumble into the abyss. Whenever he awoke from the vision, he took a deep breath and thanked God that he had not fallen, and that what had taken place in the dream had not happened here in his waking life.

Likewise, what troubled and baffled him was his inability to understand how he came to be inside the crumbling house, since it had no door, nor windows. He could not have dropped from the sky. He simply appeared there, inside, and did not emerge again until he woke up. He wandered about in the darkness like a blind man. He trembled, terrified of falling, dreading the being and unable to escape this phantom place until he awoke.

Without understanding why, he was sure that if not for the rickety floor, the crumbling palm trunks, and the gloom, he would have been able to locate the invisible being. He tried to force himself to move, but was undone by his helplessness. On the fourth day, though his sleep was no less fitful and broken than it had been before, his nightmares abruptly stopped.

Shame had planted an ache that surpassed all other feeling in his heart. Yet now, the return of the dream filled him with fantastical thoughts of dread. He was terrified by something obscure and this fear had begun to displace his sense of shame. Yet when the dream disappeared on the fourth night, it was the shame that remained.

These were restless days for Ukhayyad. He forgot to drink tea. He forgot to drink water. He had even forgotten the piebald.

He spent his hours wandering through the fields, and climbing up and down the mountain until he was overcome by fatigue. Then he would collapse and lie down wherever he happened to be—under a broom or lote tree, in the shade of a rock, or inside a cave, on the summit of the mountain or at its foot. The piebald paced after him, bewildered. While Ukhayyad climbed up mountains, the camel would wait at their foot, in distress.

Who had dared to spread the pernicious rumor that had turned the signs upside down? Who had invented this falsehood? Was it Dudu—or his wretched servants? Was it Ayur, hoping to repay the insult he had shown her when he traded her away for a camel? Or had they all conspired together in the lie? How could they say that he had sold his family for a handful of gold dust? What did gold have to do with it? He had accepted the flecks of metal as a gift, but only at the last moment. He had refused the dust, but the man had insisted. Had his insistence been a ploy? What perplexed Ukhayyad most of all was how quickly the rumor had taken flight— already it had traveled to the farthest reaches of the desert. From time immemorial, it has been said that desert winds carry with them all kinds of rumor and report—especially stories of scandal and outrage. My God—the story told of a shameful deed, the likes of which had never been heard of before in the desert. Even the lowest slave would never sell his wife or child for a handful of gold dust. To hell with the gold—that handful of dirt—he had accepted. The stuff brought nothing but ruin. Ukhayyad had even mentioned how, in his tribe, the yellow copper was considered a curse. And now its curse had caught up with him. It had caught him even though he had not done anything wrong. What they said was libel and slander, but had he inadvertently done something wrong?

He had almost forgotten the promise he made to Tanit. Was Tanit's pledge behind this—or was it his father's curse? This was enough to make his head split and his heart explode. Patience now—he needed to be patient. Patience was a form of worship. It was prayer. Patience was life itself. Were the confused thoughts in his head what Sufi sheikhs meant when they talked about the malicious whispering of the Devil? Was this what people called madness?

He had suffered patiently through all kinds of calamity, but how could he withstand something like this with mere patience? It was worse than shame and worse than death. If only he had died! No, it was better to die after he had a chance to make good his mistake. He would have to show people the truth of what had happened. He had sold no person—he had relinquished only his fetters. Of his own will, he had slipped his chains in order to win back his life with the piebald. He had sought salvation—to be free. But who would understand the nonsense he was spouting now? Who would believe these fantastical ideals coming out of his mouth?

In the end, though, he had accepted the gold dust. He had redeemed the pledge of his camel and handed over his wife and child to a foreign man who claimed—perhaps fraudulently—to be her kin.

So easily had he fallen into the trap. No one would believe his story—all the evidence seemed to condemn him. What would he do? He could not go to his death covered in this sort of shame. He would go to the bastard and wrench the truth from his lips. He would force Dudu to tell the truth to all who would listen. And, most of all—he would return the damn gold. Dudu had used it to slander Ukhayyad. The man had dirtied Ukhayyad's hands and polluted his soul. What now could wash away the stain of that accursed shiny yellow copper? Death might wash away the curse, but how would Ukhayyad wash the insult from people's minds?

He made up his mind to leave the valley. With a single blow, the rumor had killed the fables of Ukhayyad's new life. The illusion returned—as shame. The doll came back as child, the noose as wife.

The meaning of everything returned to what it had once been—with a vengeance.

27

He had no idea how he made the journey, nor how he arrived at the oasis. Nor did he recall how many nights he spent on the road, nor whether he stopped to sleep, or whether he had journeyed day and night without interruption.

Just south of the oasis, in the open space beside the palm groves next to the hut he had once lived in, he spied a group of veiled men tending to slender Mahris. Was this a wedding procession? Had Ukhayyad arrived on the wedding night?

He followed the path that wended around the green thicket of trees. At the entrance, he met a peasant. He asked the man where he could find Dudu. The farmer stuttered and hesitated, standing there in seeming astonishment. Confounded, he finally pointed toward the east and uttered, "You'll find him over there—at the vineyard spring."

Ukhayyad led the piebald into the palm groves. The man stood, watching him with bewilderment. What did his look mean? Was he staring at Ukhayyad simply because he had returned to the oasis, or had another rumor gone around that Ukhayyad had died? Had the poor man heard the story of Ukhayyad's horrible deed—was he stunned to see him show his face again? Or had the man simply noticed something in Ukhayyad's eyes? Only God knows what goes on in the minds of peasants.

From the west, from beyond the groves, ululations exploded from a distant celebration. Had the wedding begun?

Around the vineyard spring all was silent except for the crickets that began to compete with one another in song.

He heard the noise of water tumbling from the basin of the spring into small channels below. Ukhayyad walked toward it.

The spring was surrounded by a thick ring of date palms, and fig and pomegranate trees. The basin of the spring was round and wide. From its mouth gushed pure, still waters, which then poured over the lip into conduits below. There was only one path that led from this dense copse toward the eastern desert. Through this opening the peaks of sand dunes appeared in the distance.

Ukhayyad turned right. He hoped to approach the spring from the path on the eastern side, he wanted to keep the Mahri close by him. Before he even reached the pool, he saw the man's loose-fitting robes—they had been thrown over a bramble of palm. As Ukhayyad's heart raced, the universe seemed to grow increasingly quiet. It seemed that now even the trees were listening to him, thinking, observing and . . . waiting. As the silence intensified, the singing of the crickets became more raucous. He heard the sound of water in the spring—the man was taking a bath. The groom was bathing—and getting ready to slip into bed next to his wife. The man had certainly known how to steal her. He had set up Ukhayyad to act as his accomplice—and then he snatched her away. He was the worst kind of bandit—no: bandits steal only camels, but this devil steals other people's wives! This was unheard of in the desert—and Ukhayyad had been the man's first victim. But it was worse than this—the thief had then gone and told people that he had bought her, fair and square, with his gold. His slaves were his witnesses—and they would swear to it. They had already sworn to it—Dudu had been confident that people would not talk. He had been sure that people would happily accept his fait accompli. He had come from Aïr to retrieve his kinswoman—his cousin, no less!—and had used his own money to do so. Who could object to such a thing? On the contrary—they would think him a brave man for doing what he did—a hero. And they would believe that Ukhayyad—descendant of the great Akhenukhen, son of the most venerable of the desert tribes—had sold his wife and child for a handful of dirt. To them, he would be a villain stained with shame. And what shame!

The afternoon sun was slanting its way toward sunset as Ukhayyad came to a halt. He looked down on his opponent's head. The two men stared at each other for a long time.

Dudu cast a feeble glance up at Ukhayyad and stopped splashing in the water. His gaze was now unveiled. His bare head was exposed, as were his eyes. He had been caught undressed, with no veil to cover his heart. His ears were suddenly huge, and flopped around like those of a donkey. His pate was bald and eggish, and his beard was a billygoat's. His body was suddenly all skin and bones—none of this had ever shown under the flowing robes he always wore. Puffed out and colorful, this man's clothes had made his corpse look imposing. Everything about the man was a fraud. Ukhayyad now stood amazed at how easily this dull monster of a man had fooled him. His vision and judgment had been completely blinded by this sorcerer. There was no doubt about it—he was a witch doctor. Was he not from Aïr—that land of sorcerers and witches?

He opened the palm of his hand and raised it toward his head. It did not take long for Ukhayyad to aim. Never lifting his gaze, he pulled the trigger. The shot exploded . . . but missed. Dudu rose, his eyes now begged and pleaded for mercy. The man's lips moved as if he had something to say. Right then the second shot ripped through his throat. Dudu disappeared into the water, his eyes and mouth wide open, the words dead on his lips. The bullet had given him no time to utter what he had to say. As blood mixed with water, red billows began to ripple and spread, until they consumed the pure waters of the spring.

"This is a gift from the giraffe," Ukhayyad said as he opened the pouch of gold dust and poured it over where the body had vanished into the spring.

Beneath the rays of the setting sun, gold flecks sparkled in the glimmering blood-red waters.

To the distant west, beyond the palm grove, another wedding song sounded.

28

Ukhayyad flew toward the desert. His aim was to reach Jebel Hasawna in whose caves he would find refuge. He spent the first night after the incident out in the open wilderness. There, the vision that had abandoned him now returned. It was the same dream—with the same dark phantom that concealed itself in the folds of the shadows and in the debris-strewn rooms. It was the same decrepit house, still sealed securely though without windows and doors, and despite the fact that it was crumbling apart. The house was like a closed circle. And all the while, he searched around—through the chimeric hallways, on the roof that was always on the verge of collapse. As he searched for the being, for the secret, he felt a breeze on his skin. Now he stumbled, now he used his hands instead of his eyes to look. Now he avoided the imaginary walls. He could not see these walls, nor could he touch them, but he knew they were there—sturdy, thick, and impenetrable.

This final vision was not a dream at all. It had started while he was asleep, but continued after he awoke. He deliberately kept his eyes open during the dream so as to pass through it. But the shadows were too thick, and the roof under him continued to shake, threatening to collapse at any second. And although the invisible being made its presence felt, it never showed itself. This strange, wakeful state went on and on for what seemed like hours. When Ukhayyad finally sat up in the glow of dawn, his head ached. He lay down again and went back to sleep.

In the following days, the dream vanished once again. Throughout this time, Ukhayyad kept to the outskirts of the mountain.

The foreign invasion still threatened the road toward the Hamada desert, the merciful realms across whose western and southern edges his tribesmen had scattered. Ukhayyad knew that after all that had happened, his blood ties to them had been severed. And not just his ties to his own tribe, but to everybody. The blood he had spilled would never wash away the shame attached to him—only death would clean his slate. He had been sentenced to live in isolation forever. It would be folly for him to speak with any person now, or to look anybody in the eyes again. Now, his sole friend would be the piebald. He had wanted to remain by the piebald's side—and now God had granted this wish and decreed it so for eternity. The piebald now belonged to him and he to the piebald—and nothing but death would pull them apart. Not even death would separate them. They would depart together, and together they would return to their original state, to what they had been before birth.

Perhaps what had happened was a blessing, and not just a curse: Yes—with this damnation was also a kind of salvation. When a curse is eternal, it contains its own form of release: it drives one toward exile, and in exile safety is found.

But this particular curse did not halt on the frontiers of exile. The victim's kinsmen had arrived from Aïr and then fanned out across the desert, each demanding Ukhayyad's head. Initially, they were men who claimed to be his kin so as to inherit some of the wealth Dudu had left behind. The man's unavenged blood now stood between them and their fortune, for it was custom in the desert to insist that a murdered man be avenged before his inheritance was divided. Thus, they began to seek Ukhayyad in earnest, not out of any love for Dudu, but in order to carve up the spoils as quickly as possible. To this end, they had employed tricks borrowed from elsewhere—tricks the northern wastes had never known before: they began bribing herders and those nomads who knew every detail of the northern deserts. It is a well-known fact that gold blinds all and corrupts even the best of people. It was that accursed gold that led them to Ukhayyad. And it was gold—not really these men—that chased after him in hot pursuit. Is there any curse in this world that does not have its roots in that metal?

At first, they combed the mountain range, searching through the summits stone by stone. Then, they were led to his hideout by camel dung—the piebald's droppings. They set up camp beneath the mountain, and then stopped climbing through the mountain stones for several days. Perhaps they were awaiting a messenger or a command from the group in the oasis? There were three groups of them: one here, another tending the flocks of camels in Danbaba, and a third quartered in Adrar oasis. The battle was led from the oasis—at least, that is what a herdsman heading west had told him.

Ukhayyad thought about the trap closing in around him. Time was now working against him. If he remained holed up in the nooks of these parts, they would find him within a day, or a few days at most. His water supply would run out in two days, and the green grasses—that gift of the merciful rainclouds—had already begun to wither and grow sparse. The summer sun had begun its labors.

He waited for twilight to fall, then stole between the rocks until he arrived at the ravine where the piebald was grazing. He saddled the camel and placed the waterskin on him, along with all the provisions he could carry. He then set out toward the mountains. The camel galloped the whole day until they approached the eastern end of the range. Ukhayyad climbed up to the highest peak, where he hid his supplies. He walked back to the Mahri and then flung himself on the animal's neck. He gazed into the camel's deep, merciful eyes. "Now we will separate," he said in a plaintive voice. "We must part. They'll kill us if we stay together. Go into the Hamada desert, as far away from here as you can. Don't be afraid about me. No one can touch me while I'm here on these peaks. They don't know these paths and ravines and caves like I do. They are not from here—they're foreigners. The important thing is for you to disappear. You'll be safe when you get to the Hamada. When this trouble passes, we'll find each other again. After that, you and I will never be apart again, ever. Agreed?"

The camel rose to his feet. He rubbed his muzzle against Ukhayyad's arm. He licked Ukhayyad's cheeks behind the dark veil that covered them.

Ukhayyad delivered his last will and testament to the animal with their mantra, "Patience. Just be patient. Don't forget the power of these magic words. Patience is life."

The Mahri stared at the horizon where the barren waste stretched forever. Then he headed off on the long journey.

The despondence in the camel's eyes was something Ukhayyad had never seen before.

29

Ukhayyad retreated into the most rugged part of the region. There he took refuge in an unusual cave. It was actually more a cleft that crept all the way up the wall of stone to the mountain's summit. He avoided the lower caves, since they would be the first place the mercenary herders would look. The desert of the Hamada was now surrounded—from the north, the Italians sought to rush in, and from south, the tribes of Aïr sought to violate its pristine wastes. He was trapped. Even God's vast wilderness could be transformed into a prison—one more impenetrable than the Ottoman jail whose ruins he had seen in Adrar. Ukhayyad felt suffocated. He was completely stranded—and nothing good comes to a person once he is cut off from everyone and everything.

The bastards pursuing him knew this: not even his own tribe would rush to his defense. Their timing was perfect. First, he had fallen out with his father, then he had been expelled from his tribe, and then, with the gold dust outrage, there had been a final break. When his tribe heard the story of his shame, they would wash their hands of him forever. The conditions for pursuing him were ideal and his pursuers would hunt him down, not to extract revenge for their murdered kinsman, but solely to remove the block that stood between them and the division of Dudu's wealth. When rich men are murdered, it is the brutes and monsters who race fastest to extract revenge. A sense of love or the desire to avenge spilt blood are merely the excuses they invent in order to lay their hands on the spoils.

Dudu had suffered and fought the devils of the Bambara. He had put his body in the path of their poison arrows in order to seize their gold. And yet, when the man died, all his riches would fall into the hands of these cowards. That is the way of this world. It is the cowards who always remain to sweep up the spoils, and it was Ukhayyad's bad fortune to have placed himself in their way. They would not sleep a single night until they had torn him limb from limb, until they had blotted him out for good. Flecks of gold dust were all they desired. That vile gold dust. It was the cause of everything that had happened. It was gold dust that had murdered Dudu, not Ukhayyad. But was there anyone sane enough to understand this? The reasonable people had stayed at home in Aïr. Would sane people travel for months on end to chase after gold and to hunt a single man across the heights of Jebel Hasawna?

Before settling himself in the crevice, he gazed across the magnificent mountain. From the west, its body stretched out, bowing toward Mecca in the east. The living glow of the desert dawn wrapped a blue turban around the mountain's lofty peak. It was sunrise, and the mountain held its tongue. Rather than disclosing the mysteries it had learned by heart during the night from the mouth of God, it chose to write them down for posterity. The mountain's sublimity was the gift of such secrets. Is there anything more exposed or more concealed than the desert?

There are some things you can feel and never touch. Such are these mysteries, these strange ideas floating across the void, and these vague sensations now folded themselves into shadow and silence. Ukhayyad now prostated himself before them in worship. That evening, he had said farewell to the piebald and watched the animal as he shimmered over a silvery mirage before sinking below the horizon. At that moment, he asked these mysteries to deliver him from the envy and spite that now sought him. He prayed that he would meet the piebald again soon. In this silent prayer, he kept his innermost wish to himself: that their reunion should take place under happy circumstances.

But he forgot to seal his plea with the Throne Verse, or any sura of the Qur'an for that matter. He did not seek refuge from the malice of Satan during his prayers. Thus, when the mysterious powers of the desert convened in hasty consultation with one another, the Devil knew how to interfere, agreeing to speed their reunion, though under circumstances of his own making. Without hearing an answer to his prayers, Ukhayyad secured himself within the impregnable rock. He blocked up the mouth of the crevice with rocks, and squeezed his body into his new jail. He entered it in the evening and slept sitting—knees bent to chest.

It was only in the morning that he noticed the colorful drawings of the ancients. The towering walls were covered with them. To his right, a herd of buffalo spread out across a field, grazing at their leisure—some of their heads bent to the ground as they crop the grass, another group raises their heads lazily, giving the impression they are chewing on cud. To his left, the ancient sorcerers had carved an enchanting scene. A group of herdsmen chase a moufflon crowned with enormous horns. The animal runs toward a distant mountain. Some of the hunters wield spears, while others shoot with bows at their prey.

It was hard to divine the outcome of the hunt: the distance between the moufflon and the hunters does not suggest that he will get away, despite the mountain that lies at the end of his path. The painter had drawn the mountain on the horizon so as to place hope before the poor moufflon. The mountain is its sole hope for salvation. The animal knows this—and hastens with all his strength. It is clear that the moufflon is exhausted, his outline shows that. The animal's figure is heavy, yet he some-how derives strength from the unknown—the unknown that drives creation to love life. The hunters also know that he will escape if he takes refuge in the mountain—and their pursuit intensifies. They aim their spears and arrows so very precisely, yet the moufflon remains unscathed. Despite all this, there is lit-tle chance that the animal will escape.

Ukhayyad did not know how he was so sure that the moufflon would perish. He could not understand how the sorcerer artist had been able to impart that disturbing conclusion. Nor did he know why this revelation made him feel so despondent.

30

They arrived two days later.

Ukhayyad heard their chatter at dawn and thought it was just the murmurings of jinn. These spectral voices are well known on Jebel Hasawna. All who have ever stopped for the night beside the mountain are familiar with them. All who have ever passed through the mountain's foothills at night also know them well. Cowards dread passing through this mountain range — supposing, like fools, that jinn are more wicked than men! Yet, for his part, Ukhayyad had never known anything more pernicious than humans. Fearful men are best off fearing men. He who supposes people are kind is bound to be injured. He who entrusts his affairs to men will be disappointed. But he who puts his neck in the hands of men is the sorriest of all!

Ukhayyad had experienced what it meant for a man to pawn his head to a human being. He alone possessed the right to sound the warning. Who would dare to condemn humanity other than he who has learned about humans through hard experience? What person would raise his voice against humanity but one whose feet had once been in the fire? How miserable that person is! How tough his heart must be!

Then the murmurings ceased.

He stayed in his hiding place until the late afternoon. In this kingdom of silence, he heard nothing but the ringing in his ears. Had they gone? Had he been imagining things? Or was it really just the muttering of jinn? But jinn chattered to one another only in the dead of night, never at dawn. Dawn was their holy sanctuary. In the Hamada, the break of day meant that everything became mute, and jinn returned to their underworld.

He wet his saliva with a sip from his waterskin, then removed the stones from the entrance to his hiding place. The light flooded in and blinded his eyes. Like a lizard, he crawled out of the crevice. The late afternoon sun was brutal. He scrambled down the northern slope of the mountain to study their tracks. He walked in the direction he had heard the whisperings coming from at dawn. Ukhayyad had not gone a hundred feet before he nearly bumped into one of them who was crouched over behind a large rock. As the man looked up, Ukhayyad vanished behind the rocks. Had he been seen? Even if he had not been seen, his shadow or outline surely had. The man suddenly moved, scrambling over the rocks across the slope. So, something had alerted his attention and now he was in hot pursuit. The silence that had followed the murmurings had been part of a coordinated plan!

Ukhayyad crept between the rocks, hiding himself behind stones. He climbed up the slope with hands and feet. Sweat poured from his brow and his heart pounded. Only steps before he reached the entrance to his hiding place, he stumbled into someone or something—a huge moufflon ram, with matted fleece and gnarled horn! The ram was as startled as he and, instead of turning to run, froze suddenly, directly opposite

Ukhayyad. He and Ukhayyad stared at one another for a long time. In his eyes, Ukhayyad glimpsed many mysteries. He instantly understood why some men hunt only the moufflon—the animal is no earthly creature, but something divine, more like an angel or emissary. Yes—the moufflon, like the piebald, was a messenger sent from on high. Divine messengers such as these are so very rare!

He heard the roar of rocks tumbling down the slope, and realized his enemy was not far behind. Ukhayyad bolted into his hiding place, leaving the stunned ram still standing there. For the first time ever on Jebel Hasawna, it was a human who fled from the majestic moufflon ram. Ukhayyad secured the entrance with stones, held his breath and listened to the pounding of his heart. He had been prompted to jump to safety, not because of his fear of the steadily gaining enemy, but because of this ghostly encounter with the moufflon. At that moment, he remembered the exhausted moufflon painted on the wall and began to tremble.

The shot rang out. The echo bounced across the mountain for what seemed like an eternity. In places where deep silence reigns, the crash of a gunshot is even more profound. He knew this from having often gone hunting gazelles in nearby valleys during easier years—back before the Italians invaded the country and drove the various tribes into exile.

Had they hit the ram? The men shouted back and forth to one another. A little later, there was some commotion—they had in fact shot him.

One of the men walked up to Ukhayyad's hiding place and called out to his friends, "This is the ram's den. These are his tracks. These are his droppings. There are no footprints here. I don't think you saw a person over there. What you saw was the shadow of the moufflon."

Ukhayyad wept.

For the second time in his life, he was crying. He could not hold back the tears in his eyes—they poured out on their own. God had sent him a messenger, and these wicked men had killed it.

The messenger had erased all traces of human footprints in front of his refuge. He had also left his droppings. Is this what the animal had wanted to tell him by that inscrutable look? Had he been saying, "I've come to rescue you from them—so, save yourself!" My God—why did the innocent always fall at the hands of the most malevolent of creatures? Why do such people kill every messenger that is sent to them?

He listened to the noises outside. Some were busy skinning the animal. Others were collecting the firewood. One of them began to sing at the top of his voice.

31

n his crypt, Ukhayyad chewed on a few dates, all the while tortured by the aroma of the meat roasting outside. Throughout the night, the smell had risen up to the summit of the mountain and then wafted down through the crevices in the stone. Eventually, it seeped into Ukhayyad's hiding place and saturated the still air.

At the end of the night, he heard one of the men relieving himself at the door to his hiding place. Like a jinn, the man talked to himself, "I still haven't tasted my moufflon. My moufflon got away. They don't believe I saw him. I saw the ram of a lifetime, and won't rest till I catch my prey. How can I go back to the oasis without his head in my hands? If I go back to Adrar without his head as my trophy, that means I'm going back to Aïr without my fair share of the spoils."

Then Ukhayyad heard the man sob.

Ukhayyad could not believe his ears. He held his breath and concentrated all his senses on listening. He was not imagining things: the man was indeed crying. This kind of man was especially terrifying. When a man in the desert cries because he wants something so badly, it means he will surely attain it. This man wanted Ukhayyad's head—and was crying because he had not got it. My God—had his wretched life suddenly become so important? No, he was not the object of their desire—the gold was. The itinerant herdsman had not been wrong—all his speculation about them had been right. They wanted nothing but the gold. And Ukhayyad was the serpent guarding the treasure. To take their plunder, they would have to kill the serpent standing in their way. He remembered Sheikh Musa's prayer, "Lord, do not make me guardian over treasures of this world." Now he understood what this priceless plea meant. The mind of the guardian is never at ease—and the sword lies forever upon his neck.

His heart now filled with distress—this den at the top of the mountain was not actually secure. All night long, the man's weeping continued to ring in his ears. Where men suffer, there danger lies. Whenever you hear the man behind you weeping in pain, you can be sure of this: his hand will soon be upon you. Ukhayyad would not find safety in any one place. Safety would now be found only in moving—in fleeing across the wide open deserts.

He made the decision to abandon the mountain. At dawn tomorrow at the first opportunity, he would leave. During fits of sleep, he visited the house of shadows again. But at dawn, before he found a chance to escape, the piebald returned.

32

He heard the uproar on the slope as they surrounded and overwhelmed him. Loud shouts went up. Still, some time passed before Ukhayyad heard his howl of distress, "Aw-a-a-a-a-a-a."

What were they doing? The camel's bellowing returned, even louder than before and now the echoes reverberated back and forth across the mountain peak. Only then did the stench of burning flesh hit his nostrils.

Now Ukhayyad understood—they were scorching the camel's skin with hot irons. Burning the animal's flesh, they seared Ukhayyad's heart. Hawks cannot be caught unless you disturb their nests. And these men knew where Ukhayyad's nest was—Dudu's servants had led the men right to the camel. Maybe the toothless herder was among them, acting as their guide? Sheikh Musa had been right—he was right about everything: "Place your heart nowhere but in heaven. If you leave it in the care of someone on earth, it will be stolen and burnt into cinders." Sheikh Musa had never pawned his heart, nor had he loaned it to anyone. He had never married, never had children, and never raised herds of sheep or camels. Perhaps that was how he remained free from worry. In fact, the sheikh was never angry, nor did he laugh. There was only ever a constant smile on his lips. Ukhayyad had defied the sheikh's wisdom—he had made the mistake of putting his heart into the care of a friend. By placing his heart with the piebald, the hand of sin had managed to catch him—the hand of men.

Again, the cry of distress rent the desert silence. Again, it echoed across the mountains, "Aw-a-a-a-a-a-a."

His nostrils were singed by another waft of burning flesh. A scorching gust of wind carried it into his vault, setting fire to his heart in the process. The smell of burning skin became a blaze in his heart.

He removed the stones blocking the crevice, and the light blinded his eyes. He crawled on all fours, shielding his eyes. The scorching smell of burning flesh intensified as it mixed with the smoke of burning wood. He spotted the men gathered around the piebald on the slope. Some of them pulled on ropes, while others heated up knives and irons in the shimmering fire.

The smell of burning flesh was finally too much to bear.

Ukhayyad scrambled down the mountain face. Stones tore at his skin and clothes—a jagged rock ripped the turban from his head.

Wounded, bareheaded, and in tatters, he stood before them. They studied him in silence. He glared at them in silence. The old herder was not among them, and Ukhayyad felt a vague sense of relief. Without exchanging a word, the men tied him up. The piebald's body was bloodied and burnt. They had even scarred his face with hot metal and ripped open his muzzle with a red-hot knife. Blood poured from the animal's torn hide.

"Remember how Tanis took revenge on her wicked co-wife?" asked a burly man who reeked of burnt flesh.

He then turned toward Ukhayyad. "Do you remember how the co-wife got what she deserved?"

They bound his arms and legs with rope, then brought over two camels. They tied his right hand and foot to one, his left hand and foot to the other. The hefty man began to call, "Whip them, whip them!" The tongue of the lash licked at their bodies and the camels bolted—one to the right, the other to the left. Suddenly, Ukhayyad found himself stretched between the realms once more. Again, he was tumbing into the well, into the space between the edge above and the water below. Again, he was falling to that space where he had once glimpsed paradise. The houris began to trill and on Jebel Hasawna the jinn began to wail and wail.

"The sheikhs won't believe us if we don't bring them a piece of evidence," a voice said.

With bloody arms and legs, Ukhayyad attempted to pull his torn body along the ground. The camel on the right, the stronger of the two, had ripped Ukhayyad's thigh and arm from their sockets. His body was broken, yet Ukhayyad tried to lift his head.

The hefty man approached, sword glittering in hand. Ukhayyad asked one of them to help him—but was repulsed. He turned toward the mountain and, with a loud noise, his insides began to pour out. Another man walked over to Ukhayyad and gripped his bare head in his hands. The sword flew across the sky. As it moved, it seemed to perform its ablutions in the waters of the sky, in the cruel rays of the sun. Then it landed across his neck.

Across the twilight a sudden glow broke. The dream house of shadows was shaken by a massive earthquake. Its terrible wall began to collapse, struck by the blow of a sword of light. Only now did the invisible being of his dreams finally show itself as clear as day. It had finally become manifest in that moment when Ukhayyad could no longer tell anyone what he had seen.

Translator's
Afterword

Gold Dust takes place in a world of contrasts—desolate rock plateaus, lush oases, and far-flung pastures abounding in mythical flora and fauna, all surrounded by endless wastes traversed solely by camel herders, dervishes, and the occasional caravan. The focus of this novel is not the desert itself, but rather the lives of desert dwellers as they struggle against forces beyond their control. In an echo of Ibn Khaldun's great treatise on human society, al-Muqaddima, time in Gold Dust moves in cycles rather than lines. Indeed, the desert is not timeless but seasonal—with wet seasons of abundance and flourish, followed by years of drought and hardship. Human time, too, moves in this way in the novel: characters grow and wither, win and lose; caravans come and go, bringing with them holy men and refugees, riches, and misery. And always, in the background, there are the winds of empire that buffet the desert world, with barbaric French and Italian incursions from the north and reverberations from the rise and fall of African kingdoms to the south.

What may not be so obvious to English readers is that al-Koni's world of nomads is not necessarily a familiar one to most Arab readers. The Arabic novel has always been dominated by stories of the city, although peasant communities of the settled agricultural lands of the Arab world have had their place in the canon as well. Aside from the work of novelists such as Abdelrahman Munif and Miral al-Tahawy, the nomadic segment of Arab society—once so economically and politically significant that it inspired Ibn Khaldun's classic—has been largely absent from the Arab novelistic imagination.

Though noteworthy, this fact is not altogether surprising—for the historical rise of the novel as an art form is directly linked with the marginalization of nomadic pastoralism as a key component of Arab civilization. The very industrial era that enabled the one made the other obsolete. With labor performed by ever-increasing masses of men interacting with ever more powerful machines, human reliance on laboring beasts dwindled. In many parts of the world, nomadic pastoralists—such as the Tuareg of the Sahara or the Bedouin of Arabia—were the ones who used to supply sedentary societies with the animal-power that made things run. The plowing of fields, the milling of grain, the shipping of goods across vast continents—these were all ventures undertaken by men and animals laboring together. With the rise of the factory—and with it, the tractor, the train, and the car—men abandoned the society of animals for engines of their own making, and the age-old need for pastoralists came to an end. Ever since, we have only continued to cut our ties with the world of herdsmen. In the process we have cut ourselves off from what they knew, and their recognition that animals are more than just objects to be looked at, shorn, and eaten. *Gold Dust* appears in this light as a protest against the modern abandonment and objectification of animals, and an affirmation of the relationship between man and beast as one of interdependence, mutual recognition, and soul.

Since al-Koni's work is so rooted in a particular world, translation is often not so much an act of finding equivalences as of tearing something from its sense. It is not just that his Arabic reads more like poetry than prose, with rhythms and resonances that have no correspondences outside the language. It is also that some of the references have little meaning beyond their original context. To this end, in the original Arabic, the author has himself inserted a number of footnotes to explain Tamasheq (Tuareg) words and customs, pre-Islamic pagan cosmology, and classical Sufism. Rather than burden the text with footnotes, some of his notes reappear here below (in summarized or expanded form) along with a short list of English-language sources recommended for readers interested in understanding better the ground from which this translation was uprooted.

The concept of nobility—as it relates to men and animals alike—is central for understanding certain aspects of this novel. Yet its nuances are not easily translated into societies that organize themselves around egalitarian values. Critical to the concept is, of course, the idea that some virtues are inherited by birth. Of equal importance, however, is the understanding that nobility is a character trait whose weight rests on a system of social recognition. Though one may be born noble, nobility itself is confirmed by certain features of one's behavior—self-control and generosity being paramount. A failure of noble creatures—

man or beast—to behave nobly not only points to a deviation from their natural selves but also their social role—and thus poses a threat to the social order itself.

These dynamics infuse al-Koni's representation of **Tuareg** society, which is stratified, but also held together, by an intricate, hierarchical arrangement of classes—nobles, vassals, smiths, and African slaves.[1] Arguably, Ukhayyad's ambivalence about his own noble status marks the beginning of his exit from this class system—that is, from Tuareg society itself. Similarly, the noble character of the piebald is significant—as is the fact that his heedless behavior undoes the outward marks of his breeding. The term **Mahri** refers to a stock of thoroughbred camels said to date back to a fabled Omani race of noble steeds. While 'thoroughbred' and 'noble' capture some of the characteristics of the original Arabic words, the novel assumes that readers will readily recognize a difference of character between purebred and regular mounts—a distinction admittedly lost on many of us for whom all camels are equally extraordinary.[2]

The **tagolmost**—a uniquely Tuareg headdress consisting of an indigo blue turban and veil—is also ubiquitous in the novel and has its own function in the expression of nobility. As anthropologists have noted, this veil is worn by Tuareg men (not women) and has its roots neither in religious custom nor in mere practicality as a form of protection against harsh desert elements. Rather, its meaning is richly social—and is expressively manipulated to conceal (or reveal) emotion and intimacy in relationships.[3]

As he does in his other novels, al-Koni alludes to Libyan prehistory and antiquity in provocative ways—most explicitly here in Chapter 29, when Ukhayyad encounters the petroglyphs depicting the hunt. Indeed, the Tadrart Acacus petroglyphs in Libya stand at the center of al-Koni's fictional world. Some of this rock art dates as far back as 12,000 BCE and depicts lush scenes of the flora and fauna—including giraffes, hippopotami, and elephants—of the region before its desertification in ancient times.[4]

Al-Koni is also sharply attuned to the pagan prehistory (or co-history) of the nominally Muslim Sahara. The orthodox, the heathen, the superstitious, and the heretical all coexist in this world. In *Gold Dust*, it is the appearance of **Tanit**, as well as the various references to magic, spell-casting, and dream interpretation, that signal this most explicitly. Tanit (also known as Tanith and Tanis) was the Phoenician lunar goddess (and patron of Carthage) also revered by the indigenous Berber peoples of North Africa. A consort of Baal, she was goddess of war, motherhood, and fertility—and associated both with the Ugaritic goddess Anat and the Phoenician goddess Astarte. Among her symbols was the isosceles triangle, which recent scholarship has associated with particular designs of modern Tuareg art.[5] The appearance of the **moufflon**, or Barbary sheep, also has resonances within pagan pre-history, for the wild animal had a totemic, noble significance in pre-Islamic Berber North Africa.

The long-extinct **silphium** (of the genus *ferula*) was an herb known since the time of the Greek colonization of Libya and used in Roman cooking. Thought to be a form of giant fennel, the herb was prized for its savory taste, and also as an abortofacient. In any case, so valuable was the herb that it figured on coins in Roman Libya. Silphium achieved a near mythical status in antiquity when, either due to overharvesting or climate change, it disappeared from the narrow strip of Cyrenaica where it grew.

Finally, a word about two of the Sufi references in *Gold Dust*. At more than one point in the novel, Ukhayyad finds himself hanging between life and death. In the original, al-Koni often uses the Arabic word *barzakh* to describe this liminal space. While commonly translated as 'obstacle,' or 'separation,' this Qur'anic word has rich resonances—referring to the interval separating this world from the hereafter, or heaven from hell. For Sufis, its meaning is broader, referring to a point between light and darkness, spirit and matter, the animate and the inanimate. This space is not purgatory in the Christian sense, but the realm that the spirit passes through as it transcends bodily form.[6]

The novel's references to the lote tree are also replete with Islamic and specifically Sufi undertones. In the Qur'an there is mention of "the lote tree of the farthest reaches" *(sidrat almuntaha)*. According to tradition, this tree marked the farthest point to which the Prophet Muhammad traveled during his ascension to heaven—it stands at the very boundary of existence, beyond which no one can pass. With enormous leaves and fruit, the lote tree stands at the edge of heaven itself, and under it flow the four rivers of paradise. For Sufis, the metaphor of the lote tree marks the point at which the mystical seeker moves beyond human guidance and into the realm of experience itself.

I would like to thank the author and Nadia Mahdi for their help in preparing the translation.

Notes

1. See Jeremy Keenan's ethnography of the Tuareg of Algeria, *The Tuareg: People of Ahaggar* (London: Sickle Moon, 2002).

2. For more information about the history and mechanics of camel herding, nomadism, and camel saddlery, see Richard W. Bulliet's classic, *The Camel and the Wheel* (Cambridge, Mass: Harvard University Press, 1975).

3. See Susan Rasmussen, "Veiled Self, Transparent Meanings: Tuareg Headdress as Social Expression," *Ethnology* 30, no. 2 (1991): 101–17.

4. Despite its manifest faults, the best-known popular work on the rock art of the Sahara remains Henri Lhote's *Tassili Frescoes: The Rock Paintings of the Sahara* (London: Hutchinson & Co., 1959). For a detailed exposition of the problems and frauds of Lhote's work, see: Jeremy Keenan, *The Lesser Gods of the Sahara* (London: Frank Cass, 2004), 193–225.

5. See Thomas Seligman and Kristyne Loughran, eds., *Art of Being Tuareg: Sahara Nomads in a Modern World* (Los Angeles: UCLA Fowler Museum, 2006).

6. In this novel, as elsewhere, al-Koni evokes the work of Muhammad al-Niffari, an early figure of Islamic mysticism. See al-Niffari's work on the liminal points between various points of being, *The Mawaqif and Mukhatabat*, trans. A.J. Arberry (London: Cambridge University Press, 1935).